Champions of the Mists

Credits

Design: William W. Connors
Additional Design: Steve Miller, Cindi Rice, & David Wise
Editing: Cindi Rice ✷ **Brand Management:** David Wise
Cover Illustration: Todd Lockwood
Interior Illustration: Mark Nelson, Kevin McCann, & John T. Snyder
Art Direction: LN Buck ✷ **Graphic Design:** Matt Adelsperger, LN Buck
Typesetting: Angelika Lokotz
Special Thanks: Dale Donovan, Shaun Horner,
Jon Pickens, Stuart Turner, & Skip Williams

Table Of Contents

**U.S., CANADA,
ASIA, PACIFIC, & LATIN AMERICA**
Wizards of the Coast, Inc.
P.O. Box 707
Renton, WA 98057-0707
+1-206-624-0933

EUROPEAN HEADQUARTERS
Wizards of the Coast, Belgium
P.B. 34
2300 Turnhout
Belgium
+32-14-44-30-44

9559XXX1501
Visit our website at **www.tsr.com**

Life, misfortunes, isolation, abandonment, poverty, are battlefields which have their heroes; obscure heroes, sometimes greater than the illustrious heroes.

—Victor Hugo
Les Miserables (1862)

CHAMPIONS OF THE MISTS

There can be no doubt that the Demiplane of Dread is a place known for its villains. When the sages and scholars of the multiverse think of Ravenloft, the evil of Strahd, the awesome power of the demigod Vecna, and the twisted evil of the Dilisnya family come to mind.

However, this rule does have exceptions. Those who look deeper into the matter discover a handful of heroic souls who are driven to greatness by the evil that opposes them. The struggle against evils that are immeasurably powerful has been a crucible for them, hardening them into champions the likes of which no other world can boast. In comparison, taking up the sword against an evil king in a land where others will follow your example is not an especially difficult thing to do; crying out for revolution and justice in a land where no ally will stand beside you is a far harder thing to do.

Many point out that this battle against the darkness is an impossible one, and they may well be right. Certainly, there are times when it seems as if the land itself conspires against the agents of goodness and light. Whether these champions of the Mists can ever truly triumph is a matter of some speculation.

Impossible or not, however, the battle for righteousness in the Demiplane of Dread is one that only a few heroes are brave enough to undertake. Thus, the pages of this book are devoted to them.

Heroism can be defined many ways. To some, it might bring to mind images of a valiant warrior pitting his flashing steel against monsters drawn from the depths of some mad god's nightmare. Certainly, knights and soldiers have the qualities that one looks for when seeking to understand valor and courage. But the mettle of a hero is visible in many souls who never lay their hands upon the hilt of a sword.

Consider the pious cleric, who remains steadfast even in the face of great disaster and suffering. This priest's example can inspire others to go on when they might otherwise abandon all hope. After all, how many routed warriors have been rallied by a man of the cloth when their own courage has failed them? The same is true of an arcanist toiling away to uncover secrets that are best left unlearned. If the dark search succeeds, this information may lead his allies to victory. If it fails, the wizard may end up far worse off than will those who simply die.

Such examples go on and on. There are rogues who sneak into the lairs of beasts no warrior dares to face and common folk moved to acts of greatness by the dire necessity of the moment. History and lore abound with champions who never intended to become so but willingly sacrificed everything in the name of justice.

This chapter examines the motivations that drive Ravenloft's heroes on even in the face of great adversity. These characters have an important role to play at each and every stage of the adventure. Careful planning and consideration of each champion's particular strengths can be the deciding factors in any clash with evil.

The edge cuts and the sword has the credit; the soldiers fight and the general has the fame.

—French proverb

The mind is the emperor of the body.

—Chinese proverb

THE WARRIOR CHAMPION

 arriors often have a simple approach to battling evil: Run a sword through it. While this is effective against many lesser enemies, like ghouls or zombies, it can become a less reliable strategy against more powerful foes. More than one well-meaning warrior has discovered far too late that her nonmagical weapon simply was not up to the task of fighting a vampire.

In the early stages of an adventure, warriors sometimes seem to be left out of the campaign. This is generally a time for detective work and re-search, things often better left to wizards, priests, and other highly intelligent characters. This is not to say that the warrior has no part to play in this phase of the game. Her concern here must be for the safety of the others. While the wizard in the party reads through ancient tomes in search of for-gotten knowledge, someone must watch his back. When a thief breaks into the villain's lair, he needs to know that a good sword guards his escape. Even if these warriors never draw steel, their mere pres-ence can make all the difference in the world.

As the adventure progresses, there comes a time for planning and strategy. In matters of combat and tactics, no voice should speak louder than that of the warrior. Her expertise can help the party decide both the methods of attack that are used against the enemy and the weapons that are brought to bear against him.

Long before they enter face-to-face combat with a creature, warriors need to know if the weapons available to them can do the job. If not, they need to get their hands on ones that will. In many cases, this might require a skirmishing mission. By means of a quick attack or raid, the warrior can often learn a great deal about an enemy.

When the information has been gathered and the weapons readied, it is the warrior's job to lead the final attack. In the final battle itself, the warrior must draw the enemy's attention to herself in order to buy the others time to complete their plans, or she must hold back the enemy long enough for the rest of the party to escape.

THE WIZARD CHAMPION

 unning a wizard character in a RAVENLOFT® campaign requires a great deal of finesse. While some players might see the spells of a wizard as heavy artillery to back up the warrior's steel—a tactic that certainly has merit in some situations—an adventure in the Demiplane of Dread demands more of its champions.

Wizards, especially necromancers and arcanists, must constantly be aware of the dangers inherent in their magic. They deal with dark forces which, if not carefully controlled, could summon disaster. This is reflected in the fact that wizards are often called upon to make more powers checks than anyone else in the party, especially if they use necromantic spells.

The keen mind of a wizard can come into play early in any adventure. As the heroes learn more and more about the nature of the beast they are stalking, it is often the wizard's job to acquire and assess this information. Between divinational spells and the wizard's faculty for the supernatural, no character is better suited to this detective work.

In making ready to move against the enemy, the wizard's knowledge of magic and the supernatural can provide an important edge. The guidance of the wizard can often provide other party members with the opportunity to use their own skills and powers most effectively.

In addition to helping other characters make ready for battle, the wizard must also be careful in choosing his own spells. After all, attacking a werewolf with an assortment of magic designed to battle undead is not very practical. The wizard champion must be careful not to eliminate his options, however. Memorizing only offensive spells leaves no margin for error. In the event that the tide of battle turns against the heroes, a well-prepared wizard can mean the difference between escape and death—or even worse.

Religion in its humility restores man to his only dignity, the courage to live by grace.

—George Santayana
Dialogues in Limbo

He who is destined for the gallows will not be drowned.

—Russian proverb

THE PRIEST CHAMPION

The role of a priest champion changes slightly with the nature of the enemy. In almost every situation, however, the priest champion is perhaps the most versatile. Priests have access to some offensive magic, can hold their own in battle, and are even able to heal the wounded when all is said and done.

When the scent of evil first reaches the adventurers, the priest is often the first to mandate that it must be opposed. This drive and determination can also serve to motivate other party members.

During the early stages of an investigation, the priest can use her talents as best suited to the situation. If there is a great deal of research to be done, she can even turn her divination magic to the task. If the party is in danger, she can join the fighters in helping to defend those who are making plans for the coming offensive.

When the time comes to actually prepare for battle, the priest can help to evaluate strategies and options. The guidance that she receives from spells like *augury* can be invaluable in preventing the party from making deadly mistakes.

In the ultimate showdown against a foe, the priest can use her diverse talents where they may prove most effective. The ability to turn away skeletons, zombies, ghouls, and the like can enable the other members of the party to save themselves for more important enemies.

Like wizardry, the supportive nature of a priest's spells can be invaluable. Spells like *remove fear* and *cloak of bravery* can prevent a potentially disastrous rout in the face of an especially terrible enemy. In addition, healing spells can be brought into play when the front line warriors have been wounded. Even the dead are not beyond help if the priest has the power and faith to resurrect them.

Priests can also be valuable in helping those who have been tainted by the darkness of Ravenloft. Spells like *atonement* can save those who have begun to wander from the true path before they have stepped too far.

THE ROGUE CHAMPION

There is an aspect of the rogue's character that many forget. This is, perhaps, best illustrated by the character, the Shadow. Some say that this adventurer knew what evil lurked in the hearts of men because he himself had once walked the path of darkness in the past. The same is true of the rogue. He understands the criminal nature of villains and the evil side of humanity far better than an idealistic priest, a noble knight, or a scholarly wizard, since he has experienced that aspect of his own personality.

This ability can often allow the rogue to second-guess the actions of villains, root out some important secret, and strike deals with the less reputable members of society. Even the great detective Alanik Ray has noted that there is no better tool for a crime fighter to use than the underworld itself.

At the dawn of an adventure, when the heroes are often trying to figure out the identity of their latest nemesis, the rogue can be invaluable. His ability to hide in shadows, climb walls, and move silently makes it possible for the rogue champion to learn things that other characters, even those with magic at their fingertips, might not be able to.

When the party makes plans, the rogue can make sure that the enemy receives no indication of the party's intentions. His knowledge of skullduggery can be turned against those who would ferret out the party's secrets and betray them to their enemies.

As the champions' plans begin to come together, the rogue can fill in holes. If the party needs to know more about a given area, then the rogue champion can scout ahead to spy out its secrets. He can generally bypass any traps or alarms, learn what needs to be learned, and bring this vital information back to his allies. If the party must get their hands on a specific object to overcome their enemy, who is better qualified to obtain it than a skilled rogue? If it must be purchased, he makes an outstanding fence, and if buying the object is not an option, well that can be taken care of too. . . .

Once to every man
and nation comes the moment
to decide,
In the strife of Truth
with Falsehood, for the
good or evil side.

—James Russell Lowell
The Present Crisis (1844)

The Crucible

It is a brave act of valor to condemn death; but where life is more terrible than death, it is the truest valor to dare to live.

—Sir Thomas Browne
Religio Medici (1642)

A Light Among Shadows

Many people think of Ravenloft as a world of villains and monsters. They look out across the Misty expanse of the Core and see only cruelty and evil. They measure the Demiplane of Dread by the darklords who hold sway over its lands. In doing so, they ignore a great many wonders.

Few lands are as majestic and magnificent as Ravenloft. What traveler has not paused to admire the forested peaks that rise above the villages of Barovia or the stunning sunsets that paint the skies of Nova Vaasa? Is there anywhere a sight more awesome than the endless pounding of the sea against the rocky coasts of Lamordia? As the Vistani say, the Land of the Mists is as beautiful by day as it is forbidding by night.

Of all the points of brightness in this world of contrasts, none are brighter than the heroes who strive to make it a better place in which to live. Some, like the late Rudolph van Richten or Alanik Ray, openly defy the powers of darkness. Others are subtler in their efforts, opposing the endless tide of evil without drawing the attention of Ravenloft's most dangerous enemies.

These heroes have many things in common. Each is brave and cunning, although not always in the same way. Still, they have all vowed to do what they can in the service an ultimate purpose that they may not live to see fulfilled.

For all their similarities, the agents of good in Ravenloft are hardly identical. Even within a given character class, there is great diversity. The grim and determined Rudolph van Richten could hardly be less like the haughty, courtly Alanik Ray, and yet both are classed as rogues. Were they to become traveling companions, however, it is certain that their differences would serve to strengthen their alliance, not weaken it.

Assigning these Kits

The newly designed kits are similar to those presented in the *Player's Option™: Skills & Powers* book. As such, most are suitable for use by any character regardless of race or class. In certain cases, however, a Dungeon Master may rule that a kit is not available to members of a certain race or class, or even that a specific kit is not allowed in his campaign.

The following suggestions are offered to ease these kits into a Ravenloft campaign.

New Characters

The easiest way to introduce these kits into a campaign is at the time of character creation. They can simply be presented to the players when they are getting ready to enter the game.

It is a good idea for the Dungeon Master and player to discuss the selected kit before generating the character. Does the player have ideas about how the kit works that do not agree with the Dungeon Master's perceptions? Are there any rules in a given kit that the Dungeon Master refuses to allow in the game? Will other player characters find the new character a threat or an abomination? Are there variations on the kit that work better for the individual campaign? These questions should all be addressed in advance. A little understanding up front can prevent tedious game interruptions.

Existing Characters

In the case of an ongoing campaign, Dungeon Masters can introduce these kits in several ways. If a given character seems to fit a kit already, then the Dungeon Master can simply assign it right away. Any special abilities and limitations can simply be applied right away, causing a minimum of disruption in the flow of the campaign.

Human characters who elect to become dual-classed are also good candidates for the introduction of new kits. Indeed, such characters can be treated as if they were being created at the time they take on a second class.

Other players who wish their characters to take on a given kit can have them work toward that goal during or between adventures. When the characters advance to the next level, they can be assumed to have studied enough to begin making use of their kits' special abilities. This training period also allows the Dungeon Master to work a few encounters into the game that can make the introduction of the kits seem logical.

The price one pays for pursuing any profession, or calling, is an intimate knowledge of its ugly side.

—James Baldwin
Nobody Knows My Names (1961)

NEW KITS

While the Demiplane of Dread does indeed share a great deal with places like Oerth, Faerûn, and Krynn, it is hardly a traditional swords and sorcery world. With that in mind, the following collection of kits has been designed specifically for use in RAVENLOFT campaigns.

The kits in this book are intended to be roleplaying tools. They should help the player find a focus for the character, not make the character invincible. Though each kit gives the character some benefits, these are balanced by appropriate hindrances. Most of these benefits manifest as bonus proficiencies or minor skills.

These kits also give the Dungeon Master ways to motivate and guide the characters in an adventure. For this reason, many of the powers are left vague, leaving room for the Dungeon Master to use them as needed. For example, the psychic kit gives the character the ability to "read" objects. This ability allows the Dungeon Master to give the heroes information necessary to progress the story, reveal clues they may have missed, or distract them from a path they should not follow. At any time, however, the Dungeon Master can determine that these abilities fail if they detract from or inhibit play.

Each of the kits presented in this chapter uses a standard format that includes the following information.

Game Statistics

At the start of each kit description is a table that relates basic information needed for creating that type of character. In all cases, information presented in the kit description supercedes that for the basic character group or class.

The various entries on the game statistics table are broken into two groups: "Basic Information" and "Proficiencies."

Basic Information

All of the following entries list the various class-specific information that applies to the kit. This includes details on level advancement, combat, and saving throws.

Classes Allowed: This entry indicates the classes available to characters making use of the kit.

Races Allowed: This entry lists the races available to characters making use of the kit.

Alignments Allowed: This entry presents the various alignments open to characters making use of the kit.

Ability Requirements: This entry lists any minimum ability scores that apply to characters making use of the kit. The character must meet these requirements when adopting the kit but can later fall below the minimums without actually losing status.

Prime Requisite: This entry indicates the prime requisite for the kit (as described in the *Player's Handbook*). Characters with a score of 16 or better in all of their prime requisites gain a bonus of +10% to any experience they earn.

Starting Cash: Characters created with some kits have more money available to them than others at the start of play. This entry indicates the dice rolled to determine the amount of gold with which the character begins play.

Proficiencies

The last few entries on the statistics table are used in conjunction with the weapon and nonweapon proficiency rules.

Available Categories: This entry indicates the nonweapon proficiency groups to which the character has ready access. Selecting a skill from a group not listed here always costs the character an additional slot.

Bonus Proficiency: This entry lists any extra nonweapon proficiencies with which the character begins play. The character is not required to expend any slots to acquire these skills.

Recommended Proficiencies: The last entry on the statistics table presents those skills that are most appropriate for characters using this kit. While a player is not required to select these skills, it is often difficult to properly use the kit without them.

Other Information

A complete description of the kit follows the game statistics table. The information in this section also follows a standard format, as described below.

Overview

Each kit begins with a brief summary of its place in the game. This lets both the Dungeon Master and player evaluate the kit without having to read the entire entry when creating a new character.

Requirements

A brief discussion of the kit's basic requirements follows the overview. While some of this information is summarized on the statistics table, the reasoning behind it and its roleplaying implications appear here.

Description

In order to help players visualize their characters, this entry discusses things that mark such characters as unique. Of course, the guidelines presented here are not absolutely restrictive. Player characters can almost certainly deviate, at least slightly, from these norms.

Roleplaying

This is a general guide to the way in which a player should run a character designed with the kit. If these standards are followed as closely as possible, the Dungeon Master should reward the hero with additional experience points.

Benefits

In addition to its roleplaying implications, each kit presents the character with some sort of special ability. This is a solid example of the skills and talents associated with the kit that affect some aspect of game play. For example, a character designed with the monster hunter kit is very knowledgeable about a certain type of creature and gains a combat bonus when fighting that quarry.

Hindrances

This is the mirror image of the previous entry, presenting some weakness or handicap that the character must accept in order to embrace a given kit. Again, this is generally a solid aspect of game play, like an adjustment to saving throws or such.

Accursed

Basic Information

Classes Allowed:	Any
Races Allowed:	Any
Alignments Allowed:	Any
Ability Requirements:	Wisdom 12, 14, or 16+*
Prime Requisite:	By Class
Starting Cash:	By Class x 1/2

Proficiencies

Available Categories:	Common
	By Class
	By Race
Bonus Proficiencies:	None
Recommended Proficiencies:	Religion

*The requirement varies with the strength of the curse.

It is difficult to travel in a world of darkness and not step into the shadows from time to time. When the taint of evil clings to a hero, she becomes accursed. Only great effort and decisive action can save such a character from the clutches of a fate that draws nearer with each sunset.

Accursed characters are those who have run afoul of some supernatural power. As a punishment for their transgressions, these heroes have been cursed. While the exact nature of the curse varies, the general mechanics for running an accursed character are similar for all players.

Requirements

To create a character using this kit, the player must select a curse under which the character labors. *Domains of Dread* details the five types of curses that exist in Ravenloft. Two of these, *embarrassing* and *lethal*, are unsuitable for use with this kit. Thus, an accursed character must suffer from a *frustrating*, *troublesome*, or *dangerous* curse.

The player and Dungeon Master decide the exact details of this curse, but the affliction should definitely have a significant impact on the character's daily life. The story should be a creative effort between the Dungeon Master and the player, fully exploring the horror of the hero's curse. At the same time, however, this curse must not be so debilitating as to disrupt the game session.

If a hero is cursed during the course of a campaign, the character could take on this kit at that time. In such a case, the Dungeon Master could even choose to waive the Ability requirements. This could encourage the player to continue using the cursed character, instead of giving up and creating a new one.

Accursed characters need a great deal of will power. If they did not have such strength, the curses under which they struggle would have destroyed them long ago. To reflect this, an accursed character must have a Wisdom of at least 12 to withstand a frustrating curse. For a troublesome curse this increases to 14, and for a dangerous curse it becomes 16. This kit is otherwise open to characters of all classes, races, and alignments.

Description

Often, it is difficult to tell an accursed character apart from her peers. After all, the nature of her handicap is not always obvious. A warrior who has been cursed with an inability to wield her sword effectively against elves looks just like any other warrior.

However, curses are not always invisible. Many curses, especially those affecting Charisma, have physical manifestations. A character whose eyes have been cursed so that bright light is exceptionally painful might be forced to wear dark lenses over her eyes.

In addition, accursed characters often adorn themselves with charms and tokens of good fortune in an attempt to break the magical forces that burden them. These might range from a chain of garlic buds to a boutonniere of mountain roses, or even certain colors or styles of clothing.

Roleplaying

Accursed characters are generally burdened by either remorse or anger. Those who were legitimately cursed for a crime or similar misdeed should suffer great remorse for their actions. Others, those who were wrongly burdened with curses they did not deserve, feel anger and resentment for their fate. In all cases, the character's desire to rid herself of this curse should be her greatest motivation.

Benefits

By its very nature, a curse is detrimental. It is not supposed to have any benefits. Still, as Nietzsche observed, that which does not kill someone makes them stronger. Accursed heroes actually grow from their hardships in some ways. A player may select one of the following three benefits if her character

9

suffers from a frustrating curse, and two if she is afflicted with a troublesome curse. A character who labors under a dangerous curse has all three benefits.

In their effort to understand what has happened to them, these characters learn a great deal about curses and such. Any proficiency check made by an accursed character in which such knowledge might prove useful gains a +2 bonus.

Accursed characters have become somewhat hardened to the rigors of the supernatural. As such, they generally have greater resistance to fear, horror, or madness than others. Thus, they receive a +1 bonus whenever called upon to make such checks.

Accursed characters are determined to see themselves freed of their fate. As such, they have an incredible will to survive; once per day, an accursed character can draw on her inner reserves to help her through an encounter. Characters suffering from frustrating, troublesome, and dangerous curses gain 1d4, 1d6, and 1d8 temporary hit points, respectively. These hit points work like an *aid* spell in that they are the first points the character loses when she takes damage. Once the encounter ends, any remaining bonus hit points disappear.

Hindrances

The exact hindrances of this kit depend on the nature of the character's curse. Dungeon Masters and players can use the following guidelines to establish adequate drawbacks for such characters.

Frustrating curses have minimal game effects. For the purposes of this kit, a frustrating curse imposes a –10% or a –2 penalty on some aspect of game play. For example, a thief whose hands tremble at the thought of gold might suffer a –10% penalty on attempts to pick pockets.

Far more upsetting than a frustrating curse, troublesome curses call for greater penalties. A troublesome curse should cause the character to suffer a –20% or a –4 penalty to a single type of check. For example, a thief who suffers from a fear of heights might have her chance to climb walls reduced.

Alternatively, the Dungeon Master might allow the player to designate two areas in which the character's abilities fall by –10% or –2. Consider the example of a wizard whose spellcasting talents have been affected by a curse. The targets of her spells might receive a +2 bonus on their saving throws while she suffers a –2 penalty on such saves herself.

As the most potent type of hex allowed for characters fashioned with this kit, dangerous curses pose a severe handicap. They inflict either a single distinct penalty of –30%/–6 or two separate handicaps of –15%/–3 each. A cleric who has committed a murder, for example, might find her ability to turn undead suffering a –6 penalty. If the Dungeon Master wished, this same curse could instead impose a –3 penalty on turning undead and a +3 bonus to all of her opponent's saves against her necromantic spells.

Canny Dungeon Masters have already guessed that wily players may seek ways to nullify the hindrances of their curses. Doing so eviscerates the kit, as the accursed who do not *suffer* from their curses are hardly "accursed" at all. These kits are not designed for proverbial "min/max" players; they are created to enhance the roleplaying experience. Should a player character successfully bypass the effects of a curse, the Dungeon Master may rule that she has effectively discarded the kit, even if the curse remains in play.

Cold One

Basic Information

Classes Allowed:	Any
Races Allowed:	Any
Alignments Allowed:	Any
Ability Requirements:	Constitution 16+
Prime Requisite:	Constitution
Starting Cash:	By Class

Proficiencies

Available Categories:	Common
	By Class
	By Race
Bonus Proficiencies:	Endurance
Recommended Proficiencies:	Animal Handling

You might never know you are in the presence of a cold one unless you shake his hand. True to their name, cold ones have no body warmth, so shaking one's hand is similar to feeling the grasp of a corpse. People become cold ones when they have had a close encounter with undead and nearly died from the experience. Their recoveries may have been otherwise complete, yet they never regained normal body temperature or the warmth of human emotion. Not everyone who nearly dies from the attack of undead becomes a cold one; there seems to be no apparent reason why it happens to one person and not another.

Requirements

To be sure, losing the ability to generate body heat is a shock to the system. Most doctors would insist that no one could sustain the loss of even a few degrees of body temperature, yet cold ones defy both science and medicine to survive. Even so, they must be of incredible hardy stock to endure so unnatural a condition. Therefore, a Constitution score of at least 16 is required for a character to survive this conversion.

Cold ones need not be good or evil, lawful or chaotic. Common folk (and a few sages) believe that cold ones are ultimately doomed to fall from grace and become monsters, but whether that happens because of the physical nature of their condition or because they are so often cast out of society remains in question. Nevertheless, more than a few cold ones have gone on to join the ranks of undead, as if they believed that a place there had been ordained for them.

Description

To the viewer, a cold one looks like he is chilly and trying desperately to warm up. These characters tend to wrap themselves from head to toe, as though they were venturing into arctic temperatures. In fact, they are attempting to hide their condition from the world by leaving nothing exposed to touch. At the very least, cold ones wear gloves virtually every minute of the day. They may take less care to cover themselves among others who know of and accept their condition, such as among a party of adventuring companions, but even the slightest possibility that they may encounter strangers prompts cold ones to "suit up."

If examined closely, a cold one's skin has a bluish tinge. Some of them mask this coloration with makeup, especially when visiting populated areas.

Roleplaying

For a cold one, most sensations are a part of the past. Never more will the character experience the flush of excitement after a victorious battle, the blush of good wine, the heartfelt grasp of a friend's hand, the glow of a blazing fire, or the loving touch of another. The terms "warm" and "cold" lose relative meaning both physically and emotionally, isolating the cold one from those around them. Hence, they are usually extremely stoic.

However, it is entirely possible for a cold one to be poetic, forever deprived of something so basic to human nature that they cannot help but elevate it to an epitome of ideal. Such characters can be very attractive to others of a romantic bent, at least until they are physically touched. At that point, cold ones are virtually always rejected, leaving them to lament tragically about their lot in life.

Benefits

Because they have once been touched by undeath and now have no warmth of their own, cold ones are indiscernible as living creatures to undead of "Low" Intelligence or below—including skeletons, zombies, ghouls, and shadows. (Even an unintelligent ghost or vampire would mistake the cold one for a fellow undead creature.) Such monsters may still attack cold ones if their nature or orders compel them to destroy strangers or anything unlike themselves, but they always prefer to strike at warm creatures first. Should a cold one attack an undead creature, all undead within sight recognize the cold one as an enemy and react accordingly.

A cold one simply never feels cold. Any discomfort associated with chilly night air or dampness are lost on the cold one, who may walk naked in the rain without so much as shivering, let alone contracting hypothermia. (This does not mean that the cold one is immune to the effects of magical or extreme cold—see "Hindrances," below.)

Coldness permeates the personality as well as the body of a cold one. Emotions can be consciously switched on and off; normally, they are switched off. Therefore, the cold one makes all fear, horror, and madness checks with a +2 bonus. Against undead, the bonus rises to +3.

A cold one's metabolism is significantly slower than that of a normal person, causing three positive effects. First, a cold one needs to eat only half as much as a normal character. Second, if the Dungeon Master allows the optional "Hovering at Death's Door" rule (in Chapter 9: Combat of the *Dungeon Master® Guide*), a cold one loses only 1 hit point every other round if reduced to less than 0 hit points.

Since cold ones radiate no body heat, they are invisible to infravision if the Dungeon Master interprets the power as "heat reading." (See "Optional Infravision" in Chapter 13: Vision and Light of the *Dungeon Master Guide*.)

Hindrances

Just because cold ones do not feel the chill, this does not mean that they are immune to the effects of cold. Frigid temperatures, either natural or magical, still inflict damage upon them. In fact, the results may be worse because they do not realize that anything is happening to them. The Dungeon Master should track cold damage suffered by the cold one secretly, not even telling the player that the character is suffering any damage at all. Saving throws against cold-based damage are made by the Dungeon Master as well. Only the ministrations of a priest casting a curative spell can reveal the extent of cold damage to a cold one's body.

Obviously, the corpselike touch of a cold one is quite unnatural to natives and other less-enlightened nonplayer characters. The consequences of revealing this condition vary according to the specific nonplayer characters involved, but a cold one should never expect a warm greeting!

The transformation of a cold one does not come without a physical toll either. Living bodies are not designed to function without warmth, so a cold one

suffers a permanent –2 penalty to his Dexterity score. Some magical items may enhance a cold one's Dexterity, but nothing short of a *wish* spell can physically improve it. Magical items, such as *gauntlets of dexterity*, may artificially enhance a cold one's Dexterity, but potions and the like have no effect. A *manual of quickness in action* does nothing for a cold one, although it still disappears if the character reads it.

The cold one's slowed metabolism leaves him feeling sluggish most of the time. In order to sustain a normal rate of reaction during waking hours, the cold one requires 25% more sleep than other characters. Cold ones do not even regain spells unless they get this extra sleep. Furthermore, cold ones require two days to regain a lost hit point, rather than a single day.

Natural animals are understandably spooked by cold ones. They automatically try to flee in terror unless the cold one makes a successful animal handling check or uses magic to control it. Once a check succeeds, that animal will never again fear the cold one's condition, but if the roll fails, the animal will never tolerate being within ten feet of the character unless magic is used.

As warmth is an anathema to cold ones, heat feels extremely uncomfortable to them. They never sit close to a fire, and fire-based spells are extremely distasteful to them. (If the Dungeon Master chooses, cold mages could even be restricted from invoking *fireballs* or other pyrotechnical spells, and priests could be prohibited from calling down *flamestrikes*.) Furthermore, fire inflicts one extra point of damage per die upon cold ones, although they may make saving throws against such damage, just like anyone else.

Optionally, the Dungeon Master may require the cold one to undergo regular "treatment" in order to withstand the effects of sub-normal body temperature. Such therapy might be needed on a daily, weekly, or monthly basis, depending upon the difficulty level of the particular procedure. A tepid bath or a periodic *blessed* cup of tea is a simple enough requirement (unless the cold one cannot find a bathtub or a friendly priest) but more challenging possibilities include routinely imbibing an elixir of rare ingredients, rigorous exercise to keep blood flowing and joints loose, herbal body wraps, or (for spellcasters) the loss of daily spells while magical energies are redirected to sustaining life. Failure to procure treatment results in a loss of 1 point of Constitution per day, which returns at the same rate once the therapy recommences.

EREMITE

Basic Information

Classes Allowed:	Any Wizard
Races Allowed:	Human
	Half-Elf
	Half-Vistani
Alignments Allowed:	Any
Ability Requirements:	Constitution 12+
	Intelligence 15+
Prime Requisite:	Intelligence
Starting Cash:	(1d4+1) x 10 gp

Proficiencies

Available Categories:	Common
	Wizard
	By Race
Bonus Proficiencies:	Herbalism
Recommended Proficiencies:	Brewing
	Healing

For many, eremites are mysterious creatures to be both feared and avoided. Often living like hermits in the wilderness and spending their time brewing foul-smelling magical concoctions, eremites are neither trusted nor respected by ordinary folk. Indeed, the citizens of most realms draw no distinction between eremites and witches.

In truth, however, eremites are no more or less terrible than any other breed of wizard. They can use their talents for either good or evil. Eremites have no natural connection to hags or other supernatural creatures and can often use their powers to do great good in the world. Those who know and understand the powers of the eremite generally class them as something of a cross between druids and alchemists.

Requirements

In order to become an eremite, a character must be extremely intelligent and hardy. To reflect this, no eremite can have an Intelligence score of less than 15 or a Constitution score below 12. Eremites can be humans, half-elves, or half-Vistani, and they may be of any alignment.

Existing characters cannot adopt this kit unless they are willing to give up ranged spellcasting. In that case, the character could train under a druid or ranger to learn the necessary nature skills.

Description

When most folk in Ravenloft think of an eremite, they conjure up images of old crones with tattered black robes leaning over bubbling cauldrons. While this description has one element of truth in it—no eremite strays far from her trusty cauldron—the rest is nothing more than superstitious folklore.

Eremites tend to favor plain clothing. Their reclusive lives demand nothing in the way of ornamentation, style, or even modesty. As such, clothes are chosen only by their comfort and the warmth they provide.

Perhaps the only common characteristic of an eremite's clothing is its composition. Eremites tend to garb themselves in leather, cotton, wool, and other natural fabrics. Even more importantly, they do not wear metal of any type. Thus, eremites never wear metal rings, amulets, or other trinkets, though they may carry metal weapons.

Roleplaying

Eremites are creatures of the wild. They dislike the city and have no interest in society at all. They find companionship in a small circle of friends and the animals of the forest.

When eremites travel, they do so for many of the same reasons that cause druids and rangers to

leave their homes. They see a beauty and wonder in nature that must be protected, and this sometimes requires them to undertake adventures.

Benefits

In most ways, the powers of an eremite match those of the traditional mage. They can cast a given number of spells each day and use the normal spell lists.

The major difference between an eremite and a mage, however, is reflected in the fact that they spend their time brewing their spells instead of memorizing them. All of the spells that an eremite uses are actually potions that must be imbibed to take effect. Thus, an eremite who suspects that she will need a 4th-level *stoneskin* spell must brew a potion that will produce that effect when consumed. The time normally spent memorizing a spell is instead used to mix the ingredients of the potion. Thus, the aforementioned *stoneskin* spell would require four turns.

The number of potions that an eremite can have ready at any one time is exactly equal to the number of spells that a mage of that level could cast. Thus, a 10th-level eremite can have four 1st-level potions, four 2nd-level potions, three 3rd-level potions, and two potions each of 4th- and 5th-level. Potions that are lost or given away still count toward this total until they are used or the eremite "abandons" them, at which time they lose their power.

The major advantage to this type of magic is the speed with which many high-level spells can be cast. The "casting time" of an eremite's spell is 1d4+2, regardless of the nature of the desired effect. This includes opening the potion, imbibing it, and a brief wait for it to take effect.

Another advantage to this type of spellcasting is the ability of an eremite to give these potions to allies. For example, a mage cannot normally cast a *gaze reflection* spell on anyone but herself. An eremite, however, could pass out elixirs that mimic this spell to her allies while they prepare to battle a basilisk or similar creature. The imbiber of the potion is affected just as if she herself had cast the spell.

An eremite is also familiar with the more traditional magical potions listed in the *Dungeon Master Guide*. This gives her a 5% chance per level to correctly identify any such potion (up to a maximum of 75%). There is no need to taste the potion or otherwise risk death or injury in examining the draught.

Hindrances

The greatest handicap to the magic of eremites is the fact that they can concoct only potions that mimic the effects of spells with a range of "0" or "touch." In both cases, the spell affects only the imbiber of the potion. Thus, an eremite might have a draught that would mimic the effects of a *wraithform* spell but not a *slow* spell.

An eremite's brew spoils quickly once it is unstoppered. For that reason, it must be used on the round that it is opened. A longer delay causes the tonic to lose its efficiency. Also, the eremite's tonics have a shelf life of no more than one week; potions imbibed beyond that point lose "one level" of efficacy (if applicable) per week, or they cease to have any effect at all. In other words, a *burning hands* tonic created by a fifth-level eremite would normally inflict 1d3+10 points of damage. However, after one week it would drop to 1d3+8 points of damage, after two weeks it would fall to 1d3+6 points, and so on until it simply goes inert after five weeks. Meanwhile, an elixir designed to cause *invisibility* ceases to function at all one week after it is brewed. A *freshness* cantrip extends the expiration date of the tonic by one week per casting. At the Dungeon Master's option, the ingestion of an expired tonic can cause nausea, requiring a successful saving throw vs. poison to avoid a –1 penalty to all die rolls related to physical actions (including spellcasting) for 1d4 hours.

Further, a given person can safely make use of only one of the eremite's mixtures at a time. To imbibe additional tonics while the first is still in effect requires the character to roll on **Table 111: Potion Compatability** in the *Dungeon Master Guide*.

All of the potions created by an eremite are assumed to be stored in glass, clay, or similar natural containers. These are then stoppered and sealed with wax. As such, a severe blow or other trauma can ruin these spells by cracking or shattering the vials. If the residues of broken vials are allowed to mix, the **Potion Compatibility** table should be consulted. Containers other than those mentioned above (such as metal flasks) have a 25% chance of spoiling the tonic inside and rendering it inert.

FUGITIVE

Basic Information

Classes Allowed:	Any
Races Allowed:	Any
Alignments Allowed:	Any
Ability Requirements:	Intelligence 12+
	Wisdom 12+
Prime Requisite:	By class
Starting Cash:	2d4 x 10 gp

Proficiencies

Available Categories:	Common
	By Class
	By Race
Bonus Proficiencies:	Disguise
Recommended Proficiencies:	Survival
	Danger Sense

No hero lives in the Demiplane of Dread for long without acquiring a few very powerful enemies. For some, this is a passing annoyance. For others, it becomes an affliction that affects their every action.

Any number of powerful antagonists may hunt a fugitive character. Someone who has run afoul of the dreaded Harkon Lukas may find feral agents constantly dogging his heels. A character that has thwarted the plans of a secret society might discover that they are looking to make an example of him. A fugitive character might even be running from the law, seeking to clear his name for some crime he did, or did not, actually commit.

At the start of play, the Dungeon Master and player must agree on who—or what—is hunting the character. From that point on, these individuals can show up in adventures from time to time, as desired by the Dungeon Master. It is important, however, that those hunting the character are powerful and beyond the character's ability to simply kill. Once the character is no longer hunted, this kit loses its meaning.

Requirements

A fugitive character must be constantly on his toes, alert for signs that his pursuers are closing in on him. Because of this, all such characters have minimum Intelligence and Wisdom scores of 12. Fugitives may be of any class, race, and alignment.

Description

Fugitives are obviously not going to do anything to attract attention to themselves. As such, they adopt the dress and mannerisms of the society in which they find themselves. The more effectively a fugitive can render his trail invisible, the better. It is this need that earns the character his skill at disguise.

Hunted characters must always do their best to remain armed, for they never know when agents of their enemy may catch up with them. In cases where they cannot openly carry weapons, they opt for small, concealed ones—the more the better. At night, they sleep with daggers under their pillows. Hunted characters feel exposed and paranoid when unarmed.

Roleplaying

One cannot overemphasize the fear and paranoia associated with fugitive characters. They spend every minute wondering if their enemies are waiting for them around the next corner. To be sure, they hope to one day vanquish their pursuers, but that day is a long way off.

The primary source of motivation for most neutral and evil fugitives is survival. They do not care how many unwitting dupes they need to throw between themselves and their enemies to facilitate their escape. Good characters are more conscientious. If other people are somehow drawn into the fugitive's problems, a good-aligned fugitive will virtually always place the safety of the hapless innocent above his own—even if it means adopting the individual as a traveling companion.

Perhaps the only way to gain the trust of a fugitive is to join him in flight. However, the fugitive is never really sure if a new companion is a genuine friend, or simply a more cunning agent of the enemy trying to lull him into a false sense of security.

Dungeon Master Note: Roleplaying a fugitive can pose a challenge to the entire adventuring party, as the kits lends itself to mistrust and fear even among friends. Properly handling the character requires a skilled roleplayer who can balance the character's aloof personality and fear of strangers with the need for cooperation and progress in the adventure. A fugitives often refuses to go into town or to public gatherings, or he may be tempted to abandon a companion rather than risk being drawn into the open, which can interfere with the resolution of a scenario or cause hard feelings between player characters. Bear in mind that kits need not be permanent, so adopting one for just a brief time is entirely possible. It may become necessary to settle the fugitive's past at some point so the party can get on with their lives.

Benefits

Hunted characters are always on their guard. They suspect everyone and everything—often with good cause. While this makes them appear very paranoid, it can also serve to keep them out danger. In game terms, this alertness translates into a +2 bonus on all of the character's individual surprise checks.

All fugitives are also highly skilled at being stealthy. They all have a base 5% chance to hide in shadows, move silently, and detect noise. This ability functions just like those of the thief class, and thief fugitives gain a +5% bonus to their chances of success. A fugitive can also use his hide in shadows ability to blend into a crowd. This can be very useful when trying to escape from pursuers.

Hindrances

Fugitive characters trust virtually no one, though they are assumed to have come to some sort of understanding with the other player characters, or else they would be unable to work together. However, no hunted character can have henchmen or followers. Such folk are not to be trusted.

The aura of suspicion and paranoia that hangs about a hunted character also affects the morale of those around them, particularly among those who know the reasons behind the paranoia. Whenever another player character's henchmen or followers are forced to make morale checks during engagements where a fugitive is on their side of the battle, they each suffer a –2 penalty.

Fugitive characters begin play with less starting cash than other members of their class. They are assumed to have spent the rest of their money in an effort to lose their identities and pursuers.

Because of this constant fear of attack, a hunted character must be proficient in at least one small, easily concealed weapon. As a rule, any weapon of size "S" is acceptable, although there are exceptions. Among those weapons presented in the *Player's Handbook*, the dagger, dart, and knife are best suited to this task. Weapons found in other books—like the cestus, sap, or stiletto from the *Arms & Equipment Guide*—can be selected as well.

GHOSTWATCHER

Basic Information

Classes Allowed:	Any
Races Allowed:	Any
Alignments Allowed:	Any
Ability Requirements:	Wisdom 15+
Prime Requisite:	Wisdom
Starting Cash:	By Class

Proficiencies

Available Categories:	Common
	By Class
	By Race
Bonus Proficiencies:	None
Recommended Proficiencies:	Etiquette

Ghostwatchers are sometimes accused of witchcraft because they can see and communicate with invisible spirits. This is not an especially appreciated talent in the land of the Mists, except perhaps in the company of adventurers. Ghostwatcher characters seem to be inured to the sight of ghosts, and the knowledge that spirits are all around them does not appear to tax them as much as one might think.

Some ghostwatchers join traveling carnivals and perform as "mediums," some hire themselves out to those distraught individuals who want to get a message through to their deceased next of kin, some become masterful ghost hunters, and some just go insane trying to ignore what they see all around them. What use ghostwatchers make of their unique ability is up to them.

Requirements

One becomes a ghostwatcher only after coming into contact with an ethereal being. This should be no problem for a new character, but it could be trickier for a character already in play. A player who wants to adopt this kit should tell the Dungeon Master and then wait for an encounter with a ghost. Alternatively, a Dungeon Master might choose to bestow this kit without warning upon a player character after a ghostly encounter.

Ghostwatchers actually see ghosts, ethereal or not, using an ability beyond physical sight. To look beyond the ethereal curtain requires an ability to "see" without, as well as with, the eyes—to perceive with the subconscious mind and translate those perceptions into conscious observations. Intelligence alone usually inhibits the ability, dismissing what it cannot prove through the physical senses.

The trick is to accept alternate realities without proof. In other words, *not seeing* is believing for a fledgling ghostwatcher. Such leaps of comprehension require a certain amount of insight that may be found in idiots and geniuses alike, but it must be acute. Therefore, a Wisdom score of at least 15 is required to be a spirit seer. Anyone of any race, class, or alignment can become a ghostwatcher.

Description

Most people, especially adventurers, are aware of the existence of restless spirits that continue to interact with the living world, particularly those with treacherous powers. Many ghosts do little more than haunt places they once knew in life. In fact, the vast majority of ghosts are simply spirits that are unable or unwilling to continue on to the realms of the dead beyond Ravenloft. They may be people who died suddenly, those who do not quite understand that they are dead, those who died with guilty consciences, or those who simply do not wish to leave the world they knew behind. Contrary to popular opinion, most ghosts are not malicious or dangerous, taking no more notice of the living than the living take of them.

Everywhere they look, ghostwatchers see spirits, to the point where ghosts seem to be as much a part of the world as the living. Most of the spirits want little or nothing to do with the ghostwatcher, but it is possible to form relationships with some. A ghost may constantly trouble the seer, and others may even become henchmen. As always, how the character acts toward the ghost governs whether or not the spirit will befriend her.

A ghostwatcher may simply befriend a spirit, keeping an invisible companion that no one else sees, making her appear quite crazy. Alternatively, adventuring ghostwatchers might call upon the dead to spy ahead for them and provide other ghostly services (often for a price). Performing ghostwatchers amaze crowds with tricks that benefit from the aid of an invisible friend.

Ghostwatchers clearly see ethereal beings (and items) without the use of any magic. Even more importantly, those ethereal beings know that the ghostwatcher can see them. However, the dead cannot speak to the seer without the aid of special means, such as a *speak with dead* spell. Depending on the situation, the spirits may listen to the ghostwatcher's words when they have ignored everyone else, but either way, they always acknowledge the seer's presence (even if only to avoid her).

Roleplaying

Newly gifted ghostwatchers should be fairly alarmed by what they witness around them. As their ethereal sight focuses into clarity, they should be fairly astounded by the sheer number of ghosts that wander the Demiplane of Dread. Spirits pace mournfully around graveyards, through their former homes, on streets where they once walked, and in taverns, inns, shops, and anywhere else that the living may be found. Their appearances may or may not be corrupted (as defined in *Van Richten's Guide to Ghosts*), and even ghostly animals may show up. Few, if any, of them are malevolent, and fewer still are hostile toward the living unless provoked. Still, the new ghostwatcher should respond to the sight of these restless spirits as one would expect most people to react when confronted with ghosts.

However, this effect is only temporary. After the seer comes to realize that not all ghosts are vicious, the sight of them becomes less and less threatening. A Dungeon Master might incorporate the "education" of a ghostwatcher into an adventure or campaign, calling for fear and horror checks with increasing bonuses until success is virtually assured. After that, the ghostwatcher tends to think of all those benign spirits as part of the crowd. The sight of ghosts becomes so common to them that they sometimes forget others cannot see what they see, which can get them into trouble.

Some ghostwatchers become advocates for the dead. They decide their "gift" was awarded for a reason: to put to rest every ghost in the domains. Never mind that this is an impossible task, that many ghosts will repay this "kindness" with lethal force. And never mind other business; giving meaning to this ability replaces all other concerns. If a ghostwatcher heads the adventuring party, she sets the agenda for her companions, leading them on to a career of paranormal investigations and exorcisms.

Other ghostwatchers avoid any activity that leads to interaction with the noncorporeal dead; they have to look at them, but they do **not** have to talk to them. These ghostwatchers resent ghosts, as if it is the spirits' fault they can see them. In such a case, the ghostwatcher is likely to sneer at the woes of every spirit. In this case, "putting to rest" may be just a euphemism for "destroying with prejudice."

Benefits

The most obvious benefit of being able to see ghosts while they are ethereal is that they cannot easily sneak up on the hero; the ghostwatcher can spot them as long as she is looking in the direction from which they come. In addition, once ghostwatchers adapt to their ability, they need never make fear checks upon initially seeing a ghost. Horrifying situations can still provoke horror (and/or madness) checks, but ghosts in general cease to be terrifying. Neither do ghostwatchers age ten years upon sighting a ghost. (They do remain vulnerable to other ghostly attacks, however.)

If a ghostwatcher approaches and addresses an otherwise oblivious ghost, a *speak with dead* spell is required for the spirit to respond verbally. Further, the ghost may not care to talk to the ghostwatcher at all. Still, it definitely becomes aware of the ghostwatcher and is cognizant of the fact that someone sees it. Although this ability conveys no power over the ghost, many spirits that would otherwise ignore the living may be willing to converse with the ghostwatcher.

Hindrances

Many ghosts do not care to be accosted by the living, and the mere knowledge that the ghostwatcher sees them may prompt an attack. Other ghosts may be elated that a living being can see them, so they may anchor themselves to the ghostwatcher and follow her everywhere. If they are malevolent or impish spirits, the ghostwatcher and any companions can become the targets of the ghosts' tricks or anger.

Anytime a ghostwatcher attempts to communicate with a ghost, if the spirit does not immediately attack, it attempts to relate its tale of woe to the seer. Since trauma is endemic to the creation of a ghost, the stories told to a ghostwatcher are bound to be horrible or heartbreaking. In most cases, the ghost communicates its tale in a torrent of images and emotions that are staggering. Therefore, talking to any ghost nearly always requires a horror check for the ghostwatcher.

There are few places in Ravenloft where people are sufficiently enlightened to accept the ability of a ghostwatcher as something positive. Even the most sophisticated native considers the ghostwatcher untrustworthy at the least. Many people may openly attack a ghostwatcher at the first sign of communication from beyond the grave. This can be particularly troublesome if a ghost has anchored itself to the character and is repeatedly manifesting its presence in front of others.

THE GREEN HAND

Basic Information

Classes Allowed:	Priest of Osiris
Races Allowed:	Human
	Half-Elf
	Half-Vistani
Alignments Allowed:	Neutral Good
Ability Requirements:	Wisdom 16+
Prime Requisite:	Wisdom
Starting Cash:	3d6 x 10 gp

Proficiencies

Available Categories:	Common
	Priest
	By Race
Bonus Proficiencies:	Religion
Recommended Proficiencies:	Ancient Language
	Ancient History

Inhabitants of the desert domain of Har'Akir and the other lands of the Amber Wastes view the god Osiris as the protector of graves and enemy of the undead. The Green Hand (named for the fact that Osiris is believed to be green-skinned) dedicates itself to the sanctity of the grave and the destruction of undead—or those who defile the resting places of the dead.

Requirements

In order to qualify for membership in The Green Hand, a character must be a human, half-elf, or half-Vistani. In addition, he must be of neutral-good alignment and may not have a Wisdom score of less than 16.

As indicated on the table above, a member must allocate proficiency slots to master reading the hieroglyphic language of Har'Akir (treated as an ancient language) and the religion proficiency. It is important to note that this language is not the modern script used in that desert realm, but its ancient ancestor. The two have as much in common as modern romance languages and the Latin from which they have evolved.

All characters created with this kit must be natives of Har'Akir or one of the other domains comprising the Amber Wastes. In addition they must be classed as specialty priests who have devoted themselves to the service of Osiris, the protector of the dead. For those who do not own a copy of *Legends & Lore*, game statistics for priests of Osiris appear on the next page.

In order to take on the responsibilities of this kit, the character must have never participated in robbing a grave or looting a dead body. For newly created player characters, this should be no problem. For characters that have been in play for some time, the matter must be left to the discretion of the Dungeon Master.

Description

Agents of the Green Hand dress in clothing that is distinctly Egyptian in style. As such, they often appear out of place in the more traditional European settings of Ravenloft's Core domains. Even when such characters dress themselves in local garb, their complexion, accent, and mannerisms mark them as travelers from a distant and foreign land.

As it is the traditional symbol of Osiris, each member of the Green Hand must carry an ornate flail which bears an inscription in the ancient language of Har'Akir. One member identifies himself to another by reading aloud the glyphs on the other's flail. These are always personalized oaths dedicating the weapon to the battle against undead and the defilers of the grave. In combat, the weapon is wielded as a footman's flail.

Priests of Osiris

All agents of the Green Hand must be priests of the Egyptian god Osiris. While complete statistics for such characters appear in *Legends & Lore*, the following summary allows such characters to be built independently of that book.

Priests of Osiris have major access to the all, astral, guardian, healing, necromantic, and protection spheres. They have minor access to the charm and combat spheres. In addition, priests of Osiris have the ability to cast spells from the wizard's school of necromancy as if they were from the necromantic sphere of priestly magic.

Osiris grants his priests the ability to turn undead at two levels higher. Thus, a 10th-level priest turns undead as if he were 12th level.

Once a priest of the Green Hand attains 10th-level, any *animate dead* spell that he casts doubles in effectiveness.

If a priest of Osiris ever participates in or condones the looting of a grave or the desecration of a tomb, he immediately loses all of his powers and abilities and is cast out of the order of the Green Hand. A priest who dies while so disgraced rises again in 2d4 weeks as a greater mummy.

Roleplaying

The agents of the Green Hand are generally active only in the Amber Wastes. Player characters created with this kit represent those few exceptions to this rule.

The persistence of the Green Hand is nothing short of amazing. When a grave robber, or other enemy of the order, travels beyond the borders of the Amber Wastes, members of this secret society have been known to pursue their quarry all the way across the Demiplane of Dread. Indeed, legends claim that a few members have actually followed their prey beyond the Misty Border itself.

All player characters created with this kit must be specialty priests. As such, they often preside over funeral services and other religious ceremonies that honor or involve the dead.

At no time do members of the Green Hand allow a grave or other burial site, even an evil one, to be defiled or looted. They are adamant in this, taking up arms against those who ignore their wishes. Players and Dungeon Masters should note that this even includes the looting of fallen enemies or allies. The tenets of faith mandate that the dead move on to the afterlife with their earthly possessions intact.

Benefits

In addition to the regular abilities granted to priests of Osiris, priests of the Green Hand have special power over the dead. Any body over which such a character says a final blessing cannot become undead, no matter how the person died. The priest can use this ability only once per day but can affect a number of bodies equal to his experience level. This power requires the character to cast a *bless* spell on the body or bodies.

Agents of the Green Hand need not normally make powers checks when using spells from the necromantic sphere (or school of necromancy). If the Dungeon Master rules that the spell is being used for an evil purpose, however, the normal powers check is required.

Hindrances

An agent of the Green Hand always insists upon a proper burial for both friends and enemies, even if this involves nothing more than a funeral pyre. Characters created with this kit receive no experience points for slain enemies unless some sort of funeral service is held for them. Such a ceremony requires one turn per Hit Die of the enemy, as worthy opponents deserve more than a fleeting few words. The length of the ceremony is the same no matter how many bodies are being laid to rest. Thus, a funeral service for ten quevari takes no longer than a service for one. Services need be held only for enemies of "Low" or higher Intelligence.

Should the priest opt or be forced to neglect this duty, there is a 10% chance per Hit Die (of the deceased) that the spirits of the fallen rise to torment the character. Although these are always incorporeal spirits, the Dungeon Master should determine their exact nature. If the *Requiem* rules for undead characters are in use, it may be possible to translate the slain enemies directly into unique undead. Clearly, this option is preferable to simply selecting a generic type of spirit.

INVISIBLE

Basic Information

Classes Allowed:	Any Rogue
Races Allowed:	Any
Alignments Allowed:	Any
Ability Requirements:	Intelligence 12+
	Charisma 14+
Prime Requisite:	Dexterity
Starting Cash:	2d6 x 20 gp

Proficiencies

Available Categories:	Common
	Rogue
	By Race
Bonus Proficiencies:	Read Lips
Recommended Proficiencies:	Astrology
	Disguise

The Demiplane of Dread is a land of intrigue and conspiracy. This is perhaps most apparent in the various secret societies that one encounters from time to time. Evil or good, lawful or chaotic, these groups tend to have many things in common. Chief among these is the maintenance of a select cadre of invisibles.

The invisible is a keeper of secrets and a warden of the truth. She is the trusted agent of a secret society, charged with missions that she may not fully understand, but which she is expected to carry out faithfully.

Requirements

An invisible must be a rogue, but may be of any race. Her alignment must match exactly that of the society by which she is employed. In addition, the invisible must have an Intelligence score of at least 12 and a Charisma score of not less than 14.

Description

Invisibles generally alternate between two styles of dress. When hunting down an enemy of their order, they try to dress in clothing that allows them to pass unnoticed among the common folk. Because of this, they often dress in the clothes of a laborer or other average citizen.

When the time comes to confront an enemy, however, the invisible wants no doubt left as to her nature or masters. When that happens, she dresses in the most ominous and imposing garb she has available. In many cases, this calls for a hooded black robe that hides her features, making her seem somehow inhuman. A glyph or other symbol that the victim recognizes as belonging to the invisible's masters is always clearly displayed at such times.

Roleplaying

Invisibles are dark and mysterious folk, and they should always be portrayed as secretive and intelligent. If an invisible character appears to know more than everyone around her (even if she really does not), she is being played correctly.

A certain distance must be kept between an invisible and her traveling companions. Even if she trusts them utterly, the invisible must not allow herself to be lured into a position where the secrets of her order might be exposed.

Unless multiple members of an adventuring party are invisibles working for the same order, the character of this kit will find that she must repeatedly keep secrets from her companions, which can be a strain on group dynamics. If the invisible leads the group, she may have to lead them on missions without revealing the true goal. Whether she chooses to tell the party that they are serving an unknown cause or keeps them completely in the dark, hers is a burden on the heart—especially if party members die along the way. If the invisible is simply an equal (or lesser) member of the party, she may be forced to leave the group occasionally unless she can convince her comrades to play parts in her quest (on a "need to know" basis, of course).

Therefore, the invisible's distance from the rest of the group is as much a personal defense mechanism as a requirement of her position. She cannot grow too close to people from whom she must keep constant secrets. Attempts to get close to her should be met with a combination of opposing reactions: desire and coldness, simultaneous longing and contempt, or a glimpse of appreciation quickly hidden behind scorn.

Benefits

An invisible is a staunch defender of her cause, no matter what it might be. At no time does her loyalty or dedication waver.

This is most apparent in the character's resistance to alignment changes. In any case where a character's alignment is subject to an involuntary change, the character receives a +4 bonus to her saving throw (if one is allowed). If no saving throw is normally allowed, the character is entitled to make a saving throw vs. spell to resist the change.

Invisibles are assumed to be somewhat better off than most rogue characters. As such, they all receive double the normal starting wealth (as indicated on the table above).

Another advantage of the invisible is her ability to call upon the agents of her order to aid her in times of crisis. Once per month, the player can announce to the Dungeon Master that the character is making contact with her order and requesting such aid. There is a delay of 1d4 days before the invisible's new allies arrive. At the end of this time, the invisible receives one follower for every two experience levels she has attained. Allies obtained through this ability are treated as henchmen (although they do not count toward the maximum number of henchmen that a character may have) and remain with the character for no more than one day per level of the character.

The invisible chooses the exact nature of the followers at the time she contacts her society. Any type of character listed under the "Human" heading in the MONSTROUS MANUAL® tome is assumed to be available. Allies who have a frequency of "uncommon" count as two followers, while those who are "rare" count as three. A "very rare" ally counts as five followers.

For example, if a 12th-level invisible who wishes to undertake a sea voyage decides to add some of her own followers to the crew, she can request up to six agents from her society. If she chose to, she could opt for four sailors (common characters) and one soldier (an uncommon character that counts as two common ones).

All invisibles are also highly skilled at stealth. They all have a base 5% chance to hide in shadows and move silently. This ability functions just like those of the thief class, and thief invisibles gain a +5% bonus to their normal chances of success. Invisibles can also use this hide in shadows ability to blend into a crowd. This can be very useful when trying to escape from pursuers.

Hindrances

The same determination that makes it almost impossible to affect an invisible's alignment carries over to other aspects of the character's personalities as well.

No matter what steps the character takes to hide her true feelings, others still feel uneasy around her. Whenever the Dungeon Master checks for the reaction of a nonplayer character to the hero (see **Table 59: Encounter Reactions** in the *DUNGEON MASTER Guide*), the final result reduces by one step for those whose alignment does not exactly match the character's own. Thus, a result of "friendly" becomes "indifferent," and a result of "threatening" becomes "hostile." This penalty does not apply to other members of his secret society.

Players and Dungeon Masters must always remember that invisibles are not the masters of their own fate. They travel where they are told and undertake whatever tasks their mysterious masters might see fit to demand of them. This can be used by the Dungeon Master to start any number of adventures or even to complicate existing plot lines.

An invisible that violates the tenets of her secret society (as determined by the Dungeon Master) loses the benefits associated with this kit. She retains the negative adjustment to reaction rolls, which now applies to members of her own order as well. At the same time, a team of 1d4 invisibles (with total levels equal to twice that of the player character) is dispatched to exact vengeance for the transgression.

KNIGHT OF THE SHADOWS

Basic Information

Classes Allowed:	Avenger
Races Allowed:	Human
	Dwarf
	Half-Vistani
Alignments Allowed:	Chaotic Good
Ability Requirements:	Charisma 15+
	Wisdom 15+
Prime Requisite:	Strength
	Constitution
Starting Cash:	5d4 gp

Proficiencies

Available Categories:	Common
	Warrior
	By Race
Bonus Proficiencies:	Local History
Recommended Proficiencies:	Armorer
	Weaponsmithing
	Riding, Land-Based

Few families have suffered more at the hands of the dark powers than that of the Shadowborn clan. For centuries, this proud and noble line produced some of the most pious heroes and heroines imaginable—only to see them claimed by evil and darkness.

Despite the tragic history of this family, it remains dedicated to the service of truth and justice. To that end, young Alexi Shadowborn founded an order of knighthood known as the Circle. Members of the Circle became known as Knights of the Shadows. Since its inception, the Circle has been one of the few bright spots in history of the Demiplane of Dread.

Requirements

In order to become a Knight of Shadows, a character must have both Charisma and Wisdom scores of not less than 15. He can be a human, dwarf, or half-Vistani and must be an avenger. All Knights of Shadows must be of chaotic good alignment.

The Circle meets once per year at a ring of standing stones located in a hidden grove somewhere in the domain of Avonleigh (which is in the Shadowborn Cluster). Intentional failure by a Knight of the Shadows to make this pilgrimage results in dismissal from the order. Apart from this grove, the Circle has no recognized headquarters.

Description

Those familiar with the organization can easily recognize a Knight of the Shadows. Even in the most perilous of situations, a member of this society takes no steps to disguise himself or otherwise hide his membership in the Circle. As a result, they are the most famous of the "secret" societies.

Knights of the Shadows always wear plate-mail armor adorned with the eclipsed sun that stands as the symbol of the group. This icon also serves as a clasp to secure the traditional black and yellow cape that all members wear.

Roleplaying

The Circle seeks to bring the light of truth and justice into a world seemingly devoid of such virtues. They do so by opposing the evil of the domain lords wherever they can. Such activities would be almost suicidal if members of this order did not take such great care to protect themselves.

While these knights do not conceal their identities, they rely heavily on safehouses and subtle strategies to remain one step ahead of the lords who would see them exterminated. Because directly facing and defeating a domain lord is almost impossible, they often attempt to cripple them by destroying their chief lieutenants.

Knights of the Shadow are driven by a need to protect those who cannot protect themselves. Most often, this is out of affection and devotion. A knight cannot bear the thought that misfortune should come to those he loves and cares for. If he must risk his own life to keep them from harm, then so be it.

Most Knights of the Shadows have a persecution complex. For all their goodness, all their efforts to battle evil, all their sacrifices, few appreciate them, and some are outwardly hostile toward them. They take greatest pride in what they do for its own sake, not only because their code calls for it but because they know deep down that "virtue is its *only* reward" in the Land of the Mists. Because Knights do their best to hide their frustrations, they can develop stomach problems, succumb to depression (which they may never acknowledge), or suffer from a variety of mild nervous disorders. Some of them become heroic to a suicidal degree, and others eventually give up their ideals and leave the order. Still others become philosopher-knights, who see everyone as fellow victims of life, making a Knight of the Shadow an *everyman*, no different than the next person.

Benefits

Unlike most other warriors, Knights of the Shadows have a limited spellcasting ability. These staunch warriors can cast priest spells with an aibility equal to paladins do. This is a product of their dedication to truth and justice. This advantage does not, however, permit these knights to turn undead.

All members of the Circle act as the defenders of a specific group. Thus, any player using this kit must select a specific segment of the populace to whom his character is devoted. For example, a character from the Village of Barovia might be a defender of the folk who dwell in that forlorn town. On occasion, a defender might opt for a tighter or looser focus. At one end of this scale is the character who defends a specific clan or family; at the other is someone who seeks to protect his whole race or nation.

The actions and dedication of a Knight of the Shadows earn him a certain amount of favor with those he protects. This manifests in a Charisma bonus that comes into play when dealing with his chosen flock (up to a maximum Charisma of 20). The more focused a Knight's attentions are, the

greater this bonus, as indicated on the following table.

Defender's Focus	Charisma Bonus
Family	+5
Village	+4
City	+3
Region	+2
Domain	+1

No member of the Circle ever adopts an area larger than a domain, although each generally tries to protect the largest area that he can. No two knights ever allow their areas to overlap, so any given region is under the protection of only a single member of the Circle at any time. Of course, a Knight of the Shadows can call upon his peers to join him when he faces an especially dangerous enemy, but this seldom happens.

Hindrances

The magic of a Knight of the Shadows is not as potent as that of other characters. As such, any saving throw made to resist one of their spells receives a +1 bonus.

Many people, especially those who have not benefited from the actions of these knights, look down on the members of the Circle. Knights of the Shadows are seen as would-be heroes who often stir up more trouble than they resolve. Thus, the Charisma bonus that members of the Circle receive when dealing with those they protect becomes a penalty when dealing with those who live around the area they guard. Thus, if the avenger protects an entire domain, then the inhabitants of the nearby domains look down on him. If he guards a single family, then their neighbors despise the protector.

In addition to the obvious difficulties that this handicap presents, there is a greater danger than simply having a bad reputation. A person who especially despises the knight may turn him in to the agents of the domain lord. Some domain lords may approve of or disregard these knight's actions, depending on what it is they protect the people from exactly, and others may even seek to manipulate these guardians for their own dark purposes. However, there are far more darklords who would rather just exterminate any such challengers. The horrors that might follow such a decision are best left unexplored.

Monster Hunter

Basic Information

Classes Allowed:	Any
Races Allowed:	Any
Alignments Allowed:	Any
Ability Requirements:	Strength 13+
	Constitution 13+
	Intelligence 13+
Prime Requisite:	Strength
Starting Cash:	4d6 x 10 gp

Proficiencies

Available Categories:	Common
	By Class
	By Race
	Warrior
Bonus Proficiencies:	Tracking
Recommended Proficiencies:	Armorer
	Weaponsmithing

Ravenloft is a world of strange and terrible creatures, where superstitions, nightmares, and stories of terrible curses abound. Indeed, few folk in this strange land cannot describe some manner of encounter with the unknown. For many, these are simply folk tales, no more substantial than the Mists. Others, however, know only too well the truth behind these supposedly fanciful stories.

Each monster hunter stalks and destroys a single type of monster above all others. When a player opts to start playing a character created with this kit, he must select the object of his hatred. The Dungeon Master must approve this choice, and a background story should be developed to explain the character's obsession.

Good examples of monsters to be hunted include vampires, ghosts, werebeasts, fiends, and the other creatures covered in the *Van Richten's Guide* series. Alternatively, a character might stalk more unusual creatures such as illithids, animators, or gargoyles. The important thing to keep in mind is that the monster must be powerful, intelligent, and fairly common—at least as monsters go. Also, the player should select a general class of monsters (such as vampires) rather than a specific type (such as elf vampires), although a preference can certainly be established.

Requirements

While just about anyone can set out to hunt the creatures that stalk the night, characters must meet the strict prerequisites to become true monster hunters. Most important among these is the fact that a monster hunter must have Strength, Constitution, and Intelligence scores of at least 13.

While a monster hunter can belong to any class, he may be a human, half-elf, or half-Vistani. The other races of Ravenloft certainly take up arms against the creatures of the night, but none do it in so dedicated a fashion as the humans and the half-breeds of the land. Perhaps this is because so many of them live on the outskirts of society where the monsters do their worst deeds, while the most demihumans are part of tight-knit communities and thus never fully experience the loneliness and terror of such a confrontation. Though most monster hunters are good in alignment, this kit has no special alignment requirements.

Description

Monster hunters are always well equipped. In fact, they carry more gear on them than they need, just to be safe. They often have several daggers made from different, oftentimes exotic, materials; swords forged in different ways with different kinds of enchantments and blessings placed over them; maces made from obscure kinds of stone; and any number of strange herbs and items that supposedly act as wards against, or bring forth weaknesses in, the creatures they hunt. Further, players who run monster hunters should tend to make them magnets for weird trinkets. ("Sure, that bronze crossbow bolt hasn't come in handy yet, but you never know. . . .")

Roleplaying

In terms of personality, the monster hunter is indistinguishable from other adventurers at first. Like them, she is frequently on the move, seemingly something of a trouble-magnet, and devoted either to herself or a small group of traveling companions. However, whenever a monster hunter discovers even the slightest hint that her chosen prey lurks nearby, she sets aside all other business.

Monster hunters survive as much by their intelligence as their muscle. Still, once they pick up the scent, nothing shakes them from the trail. Until the monster hunter has either confirmed or eliminated the existence of that foe, she focuses her attention on an investigation that she hopes will lead to such a confrontation. This does not mean that the character rushes into the night, crossbow in hand, hoping to confront the passing Strahd von

Zarovich. Such behavior is the mark of a fool, not a skilled hunter.

Instead, the character carefully interviews witnesses, tracks down local lore about the creature, explores reported lairs, and gathers information on her enemy, its tactics, powers, and possible whereabouts. It is not until she has exhausted all sources of information that he prepares to face the creature in mortal combat.

Benefits

The monster hunter knows far more about her quarry than the average adventurer. In any given situation, she has a feeling for what the monster will do. This experience provides the character with a +2 bonus on any proficiency or ability check that directly deals with the chosen enemy. This includes the tracking proficiency that is automatically available to characters with this kit.

In combat, the monster hunter's knowledge is helpful as well. Whenever such a character attacks her hated prey, she gains a +2 bonus on all damage rolls due to knowledge of her foe's vulnerabilities.

Hindrances

Though these characters are known as monster hunters, sometimes they become the hunted. The relationship of these characters to their prey is much like that of a champion chess player to an opponent. Each move, response, and clash is carefully engineered to bring about an ultimate victory.

As a monster hunter's reputation grows, her enemies begin to study her as she studies them. Thus, the monster is often ready for the hunter when they come face to face. Because of this, her chosen enemy receives a +2 initiative bonus in any combat in which the monster hunter is the subject of its attack. This penalty applies only to the monster hunter's chosen prey. All other combatants attack normally.

As mentioned earlier, monster hunters tend to carry more equipment with them than they need. Due to this tendency, all characters created with this kit must maintain an encumbrance load of no less than "moderate." Thus, a monster hunter with a Strength score of 15 must carry at least eighty-six pounds worth of equipment with her.

Obviously, the Dungeon Master should waive this requirement at appropriate times. If the character is going to attend an elegant reception at the house of a nobleman, she should clearly not arrive with a loaded backpack thrown over her shoulder. Of course, the horse that she rode to the party on might well have a saddlebag or two thrown over it, and she may have at least one silver dagger or enchanted amulet hidden somewhere on her person—just to be on the safe side, of course.

Another hindrance to the monster hunter is the inevitable, albeit occasional, lack of favored enemies to hunt and kill. Sometimes a vampire hunter cannot find a single vampire to track and kill, especially if the quest at hand does not involve a bloodsucker. The skills and mindset required to hold mastery over the pursuit of a particular creature must be constantly honed, updated, and perfected—especially in the Demiplane of Dread—and like a musician, a monster hunter who does not practice routinely gets rusty in a hurry. Therefore, a monster hunter who fails to actively engage in tracking and killing her chosen prey for more than a week at a time temporarily loses some of the benefits of the kit, reducing all kit-based bonuses to +1. Luckily, once the monster hunter is back on the trail of her chosen nemesis, her skills sharpen within 1d20 hours of active pursuit. Note that finding and studying (daily) a book containing any information about the hunter's quarry constitutes the use of the kit skills, regardless of whether there is an active hunt in progress.

Order of the Guardian

Basic Information

Classes Allowed:	Any Priest
Races Allowed:	Any
Alignments Allowed:	Any Good
Ability Requirements:	Constitution 15+
	Wisdom 17+
Prime Requisite:	Wisdom
Starting Cash:	3d6 x 10 gp

Proficiencies

Available Categories:	Priest
	By Race
Bonus Proficiencies:	Ancient History
Recommended Proficiencies:	Spellcraft
	Religion

The Order of the Guardians is a monastic organization that exists throughout the domains of Ravenloft. This reclusive order is devoted to the discovery and destruction of evil magical items. Each monastery or retreat is dedicated to a single powerful magical device, relic, or artifact. The brothers and sisters of this order dedicate their lives to researching and understanding the devices they guard and ensuring that they do not find their way into the general population. Some items are all but impossible to destroy, but these guardians often devote much of their research and meditation to just that end.

Each monastery is an independent unit, and they rarely communicate with each other. There can even be several operating independently in the same domain, dedicated to protecting the populace from separate artifacts. Each group takes its own name, often influenced by the artifact it guards, thus concealing that a greater order exists.

The two oldest retreats of this order were founded in Markovia. The Monastery of the Lost guards the *Table of Life*. This large slab of marble keeps any body placed upon it alive regardless of the tortures and pain inflicted. The evil lord of this domain, Frantisek Markov, used this table to aid in his fiendish experiments. The other group of monks guards the *Tapestry of Dark Souls*; this sect is known only as the Guardians. (For a description of the tapestry and the former head of this particular monastery, see the entry on Brother Dominic on page 41.)

The Order of the Guardians often sends out its agents in search of dangerous magical items. Once in the hands of the order, these objects are carefully studied. If a way can be found to destroy the item, then its peril is forever ended. If it is beyond the power of the group to eliminate the dangerous relic, it is secured in a sanctuary where it can do no harm.

Requirements

In order for a character to make use of this kit, he must have a minimum Constitution score of 15 and a Wisdom of not less than 17. He must be a priest but may be of any race and any good alignment. Becoming a guardian does not affect the priest's normal spellcasting abilities.

Description

The Order of the Guardians is a monastic organization, with all members taking certain vows and oaths. Among these sacred promises is the commitment to abandon individuality. To that end, all members of the order wear the same heavy robes of gray wool. In most cases, the hoods of these robes are drawn up, all but hiding the wearer's features in dark shadows.

The robes worn by these monks are unadorned as a sign of their humility and devotion. They make use of no other icons or signs to identify themselves to each other, even when traveling in the outside world.

Roleplaying

Members of this order should always be aware of the danger presented by the objects that they seek. Although they may be able to resist the desire to possess and wield the relics they hunt, they know that others are not always so fortunate. They must always be wary of betrayal by those who have fallen victim to a supernaturally imposed desire for power and magic.

These monks possess a great deal of knowledge about the occult and its artifacts. They are, however, very cautious about sharing this information with others. As a result, many guardians seem to have a smug attitude which others find offensive.

Curiosity is a common weakness among guardians, though some of them might consider it their greatest strength. To some extent, they are protectors of powerful and evil objects specifically because they could not resist investigating the items themselves. When their searches led them to dark discoveries, their consciences made them responsible for what they had found, so they became guardians. For many, their fate has failed to teach them not to be so inquisitive. Who better to seek out and contain the terrible unknown than someone with previous experience in such matters?

Benefits

No one chooses the path of the Order of the Guardian. Those who don the gray robes of this order do so because they must—because they have the "calling." In addition to dictating the course of one's life, this calling results in several game effects.

Brothers and sisters of this order have a natural resistance to magical spells from the wizard school of enchantment/charm and the priest charm sphere. In game terms, this functions as magic resistance equal to 5% per level of the character (up to a maximum of 75%). Thus, a 12th-level monk would have a 60% magic resistance when targeted with spells from the charm sphere. In the case of characters that already have a natural resistance to such spells, the most advantageous resistance applies. This magic resistance also applies to psionic powers that mimic the

aforementioned spells. Other powers may or may not be affected, as determined by the Dungeon Master. The character may freely waive this resistance at any given time.

Monks of this order know a great deal about the history and lore associated with Ravenloft's most infamous and dangerous artifacts. This knowledge is reflected in a skill similar to the bard's ability to "know a little bit of everything." In the case of these characters, however, it applies to only magical objects, artifacts, and relics. In game terms, this gives the guardian a 5% chance per level to know something about any notable magical item that he examines. Thus, a 6th-level member of the Order of the Guardian who comes upon the *Sword of Arak* would have a 30% chance of realizing what it is.

Hindrances

Joining the Order of Guardians requires a character to make certain vows. Among these are various oaths of poverty and obedience. In game terms, these vows are similar to those of a paladin. Thus, a character using this kit may possess one suit of magical armor, one magical shield, no more than two magical weapons, and a maximum of only four other magical items.

Whenever one of these monks receives money, 10% of it must be immediately tithed to the order. Thus, if he were rewarded with one thousand gold pieces for an adventure in Lamordia, one hundred of this would be deducted to account for this obligation.

Even after this tithing, a member of this order never retains wealth. Such characters keep only as much gold as they need to sustain themselves. All other moneys must be turned over to the order. Assume that the above character spends three hundred of his remaining nine hundred gold pieces on equipment, provisions, training, and the like. He now has six hundred gold pieces left. Keeping a small fraction for unexpected expenses (10% is a good rule of thumb), he should turn the rest over to the order.

The Order of the Guardians is primarily hermetic. As such, these monastic wardens have little chance to learn the skills that others might consider commonplace. This is reflected in the fact that they do not have free access to the proficiencies of the Common group. A character who wishes to master the heraldry skill must allocate 2 slots for it instead of the normal 1 (one for the skill itself and one for access to the Common category).

PISTOLEER

Basic Information

Classes Allowed:	Any
Races Allowed:	Gnome
	Half-Elf
	Halfling
	Half-Vistani
	Human
Alignments Allowed:	Any
Ability Requirements:	Dexterity 15+
	Intelligence 12+
Prime Requisite:	By Class
Starting Cash:	By Class

Proficiencies

Available Categories:	Common
	By Class
	By Race
Bonus Proficiencies:	Weather Sense
Recommended Proficiencies:	Gunsmithing

The pistoleer is someone who has devoted time and effort to mastering *smokepowder* weapons, the highest achievement of technical warfare in Ravenloft. Pistoleers are not exactly a common sight on the Demiplane of Dread, but in the more techno-logically advanced domains in the northwestern part of the Core, their numbers are growing.

Requirements

Many of Ravenloft's player character races avoid *smokepowder* weapons for a variety of reasons. While dwarves are starting to find a use for *smokepowder* in their mining efforts, they view those who wield muskets and pistols as cowardly and lazy. Elves tend to find *smokepowder* weapons, which make roaring explosions and fill the air with foul-smelling blue smoke when fired, aesthetically repulsive. Thus, they typically shy away from everything related to them. The use of firearms is likewise virtually unheard of among the Vistani tasques, both because *smokepowder* weapons lack even a hint of poetry and beauty and because their travels take them to domains where such weapons might be misconstrued as some form of black magic.

For these reasons, pistoleers must be human, half-elf, half-Vistani, or gnome. These are the most progressive and open-minded peoples of the Demiplane.

As explained in the rules section governing *smokepowder* weapons (see page 31), no character can use any of these devices without having at least one weapon proficiency slot devoted to a *smokepowder* weapon. Since pistoleers devote themselves primarily to the smaller, more graceful snaplock and wheellock pistols, they must devote that proficiency to a pistol.

A high degree of hand-eye coordination is particularly important with *smokepowder* weapons, where the difficult nature of reloading the weapon in combat makes each shot *really* count. This same complication necessitates high manual deftness and technical aptitude. For this reason, a pistoleer must have a Dexterity score of 15 or better, and an Intelligence score of 12 or better.

Description

The primary distinguishing feature of a pistoleer is her *smokepowder* weapon. A character of this type is rarely seen in public without at least one pistol shoved through her belt, except where it might be socially unacceptable to go armed. Many pistoleers also tend to carry several small wooden containers, typically attached to a belt or sash, that hold premeasured *smokepowder* charges for their weapons. They also usually carry several pouches of bullets. Pistoleers tend to smell of *smokepowder*, and the substance usually leaves their fingers or gloves stained.

There is no particular style of dress that sets pistoleers apart. The majority of them tend to be from the ranks of the Demiplane's elite, so their dress may be a bit finer than that of the average person.

Roleplaying

No one personality sums up the pistoleer. These characters come from all walks of life and belong to all classes. A ranger pistoleer might have mastered *smokepowder* weapons in the hopes of becoming a more effective hunter for his village, while a mage pistoleer might seek to understand the technology in order to create magical bullets that can slay creatures of the night. A pistoleer who heads up a city militia may master *smokepowder* weapons due to the shockingly loud noises they make and the dramatic impact their projectiles can inflict on a single target. Finally, a young dilettante from Richemulot may attempt to master *smokepowder* weapons because, once prepared and loaded, they are relatively easy to use and thus make good defensive weapons for characters that are otherwise rather unskilled in fighting.

The one characteristic that all pistoleers share is their love of *smokepowder* weapons. Whether they use them for sport, defense, or monster-hunting purposes, they love nothing more than swapping tales of their experiences with other pistoleers.

This love of guns often transcends other biases. A conservative noble from Lamordia might find typical half-elves repulsive, but for a half-elf pistoleer, she might well put aside her bigotry and explore their common experiences with guns.

Benefits

Weather is extremely important to pistoleers. They need to know if it is going to rain so they can take special precautions to keep their *smokepowder* dry or perhaps even leave their pistols at home and use more conventional weapons or magic that day. Since they are so conscious of weather conditions, they receive the weather sense nonweapon proficiency for free. Additionally, they make all weather sense checks at a +2 bonus anywhere in the Demiplane of Dread. (This bonus negates the –2 penalty for use outside of the character's home domain that is mentioned on page 284 of *Domains of Dread*.)

With other pistoleers, these characters receive a +1 modifier to all Charisma-based checks and actions. This works even with characters who might otherwise be considered a foe, unless engaged in direct combat.

Finally, pistoleers start play with a free wheellock belt pistol. When using this, or any other pistol, the pistoleer is much quicker than other characters. For this reason, the pistols have a weapon speed factor of only 7 for these characters.

Hindrances

Due to the cultural bias against *smokepowder* weapons, the pistoleer receives a –1 penalty on all Charisma checks involving elves, Vistani, and dwarves.

When traveling away from home, the pistoleer must always carry at least one *smokepowder* weapon with him, and should attempt to have at least one charge of *smokepowder* and one bullet on his person at all times. He must also travel with the equipment and materials necessary to create more bullets. Should he ever lose these items, he must try to replace them as soon as possible.

Firearms In Ravenloft

Although "*smokepowder* weapons" (or "firearms" as they are often called) are no match for a wizard's *fireball* spell (or even the *magic missile* spell, for that matter), they nonetheless enjoy some popularity among adventuring men and women in Ravenloft.

Smokepowder is described in the *Dungeon Master Guide* in Appendix Three: Magical Item Descriptions. Despite the fact that *smokepowder* is magical, the bullets are not. Thus, they do not inflict damage on creatures hit only by magical weapons.

Smokepowder Proficiencies

Smokepowder weapon proficiencies and the gunsmithing nonweapon proficiency are suitable only for native Ravenloft characters from the domains of Borca, Dementlieu, Invidia, Lamordia, Mordent, Nosos, Paridon, Richemulot, and the western part of Necropolis. For those characters, the use of firearms is considered a Common proficiency, as defined in *Domains of Dread*. (This means that characters from those domains—of any race or class—can acquire the proficiency.) For all others, the proficiency is considered Uncommon, thus costing one additional proficiency slot.

Some of these descriptions are based on proficiencies that have appeared in older AD&D® products. For the purposes of characters being created for RAVENLOFT campaigns, however, the rules here take precedence.

All rules governing weapon proficiencies mentioned in *Domains of Dread* apply to firearms, except that specialization does not give a character multiple attacks.

Loading and operating a musket or pistol is a complicated process, and only a skilled individual can do so correctly. Thus, in order to use any type of firearm, the character must be proficient in at least one weapon of its type.

Gunsmithing (2 slots, Wisdom –3): Characters with this nonweapon proficiency can build and repair snaplock muskets and pistols and make bullet molds. If the proficiency check for building fails, the weapon is damaged, and it explodes the first time it is used, causing 1d8 points of damage to the user. Any failed repair check indicates that the character breaks something in the firearm being fixed, necessitating two subsequent successful checks to repair it.

Smokepowder Weapons

Four main categories of *smokepowder* weapons exist in the Demiplane of Dread, not including the arquebus, which is considered too primitive by the technologically advanced domains and too unreliable by the more primitive domains.

Regardless of category, reloading *smokepowder* weapons is a cumbersome and complex process that requires a fair amount of concentration. In order to successfully reload a *smokepowder* weapon during the stress of combat, a character must make a successful Intelligence check. If the check is unsuccessful, the weapon misfires. (See next page for more information on misfires.)

Smokepowder weapons in Ravenloft all share certain similarities: They all rely on packed charges of *smokepowder* to fire a front-loaded projectile. Typically, a firearm of any type can fire only once before needing to be reloaded. It is conceivable that a gunsmith of great skill or vision may create a double-barreled weapon, but in such a case, each barrel requires a separate *smokepowder* charge and a separate projectile.

All *smokepowder* weapons have a speed factor of 10, but if the character has a full round to prepare after the weapon is loaded (so that the weapon is in firing position at the beginning of the round), its speed factor is 1. Firearms are considered piercing weapons.

Characters who carry *smokepowder* weapons must specify how many charges of powder and how many bullets they are carrying.

Matchlock Calivers: Matchlock calivers are large muzzleloaders that rely on a slow-burning match to ignite a power charge. Roughly five feet in length, they are military weapons used almost exclusively by elite troops in Borca and Richemulot, and by caravan guards in Invidia. They are also occasionally found in the possession of lesser adventuring parties.

Reloading a matchlock weapon is particularly difficult. Not only must the various accoutrements be kept separate, but also the slow match must be kept lit *and* it must not touch anything highly flammable. The slow match burns at a rate of one inch per turn.

Wheellock Belt Pistols and Horse Pistols: Military officers, gentry, and experienced adventurers from Lamordia, Borca, Invidia, Mordent, and western Necropolis favor the wheellock pistol designs. The wheellock replaces the slow match with a spring-wound wheel. Pulling the trigger releases the wheel, which spins against a flint and sprays sparks into the priming pan,

igniting the *smokepowder*. Loading and reloading these weapons is still a complicated process though.

The belt pistols are small enough to be carried stuck through a character's belt or waistband, and can easily be concealed beneath a cloak. They are fast replacing daggers as the weapon of choice for personal defense in Invidia. It is also a favorite among mages who need a little extra security.

The horse pistol is larger, up to eighteen inches long. It was developed for use by King Azalin's mounted border guards, who used to patrol the blood-soaked frontier between that northern nation and Falkovnia. The soldiers would typically carry them in holsters slung over their saddles. Horse pistols are fitted with a large ball at the bottom of the grip. The ball makes it less likely that the weapon would be dropped when drawn on a moving horse and also makes it an effective club, in which case it inflicts 1d6 points of damage.

Snaplock Muskets and Pistols: The snaplocks are the most sophisticated *smokepowder* weapons available. They are both safer and easier to use than either matchlocks or wheellocks. Snaplocks are mainly sporting weapons, and are used most commonly by the wealthy elite of Borca, Richemulot, Mordent, and Dementlieu.

Game Rules

Some additional rules apply to the use of *smokepowder* weapons.

Range Modifiers: Firearms use normal range modifiers (–2 at medium range, –5 at long range). These modifiers do not double.

Armor Classes: The great advantage of *smokepowder* weapons is their ability to punch through armor. At short range, all armor is ignored; the target's Armor Class depends entirely on Dexterity and cover. At medium range, the target's Armor Class (including armor benefits) suffers a +5 penalty. At long range, the target suffers a +2 Armor Class penalty.

These penalties apply only to that portion of the character's Armor Class that comes from wearing armor; Dexterity bonuses are unaffected. The penalty cannot make a character's Armor Class worse than if he was wearing no armor.

Additional Damage: No matter what sort of *smokepowder* weapon is being used, any time a player rolls the maximum value on the damage die, he rolls again and adds the results together. He keeps rolling until he no longer rolls the maximum value on the die.

Missing Fire: For various reasons, *smokepowder* weapons occasionally misfire. If the attack roll is a 1, the weapon does not fire. It cannot be fired again until at least ten rounds are spent clearing the charge from the barrel, cleaning, and reloading the piece.

The Danger of *Smokepowder*: If a character takes any fire damage (such as from a *fireball* or *burning hands* spell), he must roll a item saving throw for whatever containers hold *smokepowder*. If the saving throw fails, the *smokepowder* ignites and inflicts 1d2 points of damage on the character for every charge carried.

New Weapons

The following equipment and weapons are available from gunsmiths in domains of a Renaissance cultural level.

A bullet mold makes a single bullet, and a *smokepowder* flask contains ten charges.

Item	RoF	Weight (lbs.)	Size	Range (yds.)	Damage	Price
Matchlock Caliver	1/2	11	M	40/80/240	1d8/1d8	300 gp
Snaplock Musket	1/2	14	M	70/130/390	1d12/1d12	850 gp
Snaplock Belt Pistol	1/2	3	S	15/30/45	1d8/1d8	450 gp
Wheellock Belt Pistol	1/2	3	S	15/30/45	1d8/1d8	180 gp
Wheellock Horse Pistol	1/2	4	S	20/40/60	1d10/1d10	350 gp
Bullets (10)	—	0.25	—	—	—	1 gp
Bullet Mold	—	2	—	—	—	30 gp
Smokepowder (Flask)	—	0.5	—	—	—	100 gp
Slow Match (10 ft.)	—	—	—	—	—	1 gp

Psychic

Basic Information

Classes Allowed:	Any
Races Allowed:	Any
Alignments Allowed:	Any
Ability Requirements:	Intelligence 14+
Prime Requisite:	Intelligence
Starting Cash:	By Class

Proficiencies

Available Categories:	Common
	By Class
	By Race
Bonus Proficiencies:	Direction Sense
Recommended Proficiencies:	Astrology

Psychics in the Land of the Mists are simultaneously gifted and cursed. Their powers allow them to peer beyond the physical and the present moment, yet there are many things in Ravenloft that no sane creature would ever want to see. Possessed of a power wielded by very few, a power with great promise and potential, psychics seem unable to resist looking beyond the pale, so they are frequently emotionally scarred from a very young age. These psychics are as often claimed by despair as by claws and weapons. Those who freely call upon their mental powers in the Demiplane of Dread should be considered suicidal or insane—or both.

The "gift" of psychic power knows no race or class. There does not seem to be any connection between psychic and their heritage or upbringing. Neither can one train in the mental art. Except in rare cases, where psychic powers are conveyed upon a person through extraordinary and usually unforeseen means, one is either born with the ability or without it. On the other hand, a person may have latent psychic abilities that are never discovered until some traumatic experience causes them to surface, or until another psychic recognizes and cultivates these skills.

Requirements

Intelligence is the primary attribute of a psychic character, so this kit demands an Intelligence score of no less than 14. Characters of any race or class may take this kit as long as they satisfy the Intelligence requirement. Alignment is not a bar to psychic ability, but it may significantly affect the psychic's attitude toward these special talents, and the willingness to call upon them.

Description

True psychics normally avoid identification because many people are frightened of them. Thus, psychics are not distinguished by any particular style of dress or equipment. Unlike spellcasters, psychics are not forbidden to wear metal (unless the character's class states otherwise). A warrior in plate mail is just as likely to be a psychic as a priest in robes or a thief in black leather.

Roleplaying

Psychics in Ravenloft do not appreciate their innate power as much as they might if they lived in another world. Each time they touch an object and try to pick up its psychic resonance, they take a chance that a shocking sight may assault their minds. In fact, the nature of the Demiplane of Dread makes such occurrences quite likely.

Just the same, psychics rarely put their powers aside, although they commonly swear that they want to. A certain compulsion to use the power rules over their better judgment, and they often find themselves reaching out to touch an object without thinking. Indeed, the mind clears of all present thought at the moment of contact, so psychics often find themselves immersed in a vision even when they did not mean to invoke their abilities.

Therefore, psychics are understandably a bit tense. They usually have either a grim sense of humor or none at all, and mirth is often a sign that they are slipping into insanity. In addition, they tend to treat everyone else like unfallen innocents, not necessarily in a condescending manner but certainly with a little envy.

Despite their lack of humor, psychics tend to be highly emotional people. Their sheer sensitivity permeates their personalities, often predisposing them to outwardly exhibit their inner feelings. If traveling with an adventuring party, they thrive on the support of their companions and express their emotions freely, positive or negative. Once psychics make a friend, they become friends for life. They are excellent listeners, and they almost always have advice for anyone within earshot. Others may find the psychics' abilities fascinating or useful, but to ask them to invoke their powers is offensive for even the best of reasons. If the psychic perceives an opportunity to use these powers to advantage, *he* must be the one to offer them; requests are met with any reaction from simple and frank refusal to outrage, depending on the nature of the request and who is asking. If the psychic can deny the existence of his paranormal talents, he will, even if it makes a liar out of his friend. In short, the psychic ability is *extremely* personal.

Benefits

A psychic is able to pick up psychic resonances by touching objects and people, similar to the psionic ability of object reading. The power is not to be confused with scrying, where specific objects and people are sought out through concentration. Rather, touching an object may reveal random glimpses of a moment in its past or future. Such visions take a minimum of one round to manifest (depending on the intensity) and have a dreamlike quality to them.

When a psychic touches an item, it may or may not be "psychically charged." This is *completely* up to the Dungeon Master. Most items and people are not charged at all, so touching them provokes no vision whatsoever. Thus, psychics need not go through life assaulted by constant visions brought on by everything they touch. A character can consciously try to "read" an object only once. However, the Dungeon Master can have new images flash in the character's mind whenever the situation warrants.

For example, a psychic cannot touch a sword and witness an entire battle in which it was employed. More likely, he receives a vision of a killing blow, the sword's wielder being slain, or even something completely mundane such as the anvil and the blacksmith's descending hammer.

Obviously, psychics can be extremely useful for picking up important clues in an adventure. Touching an object—including a dead body—might reveal the identity of the person or creature that last touched it, it might provide a glimpse of what passed there some time ago, or it might provide warning of a crucial event that has yet to occur. Then again, it might provide something completely useless, or nothing at all.

Physically touching a living creature results in an innate ability to detect evil intent (per the paladin ability). However, creatures or at least average Intelligence can sense the mental "touch" of the psychic with a successful Intelligence check. Creatures capable of magically masking their thoughts can automatically conceal their evil intentions, and the sensitive will not be aware of the deception.

Entering a site of past violence or terror—any place that is highly charged with psychic energy, like an old battlefield or a murder scene—is an extremely emotional experience for a psychic. Different psychics display completely different reactions to obviously psychically charged areas, but every one of them experiences a powerful mix of anticipation and dread when they first lay eyes on the site.

Characters who take on this kit automatically gain the direction sense proficiency. In addition, they often have an uncanny knack for finding places. While this ability never allows them to trace the shortest distance between themselves and the final encounter of an adventure, it does allow them to quickly determine the direction of many common sites without ever asking for directions. If the adventuring party is looking for a blacksmith, a sensitive can lead the group in the direction of a smithy even in a town to which they have never been.

The character's Wisdom score also affects how they react to certain visions and impressions they receive. The difference between the character's Wisdom and Intelligence scores creates a modifier for any fear, horror, and madness checks that result from the employment of psychic powers. If the character's Wisdom is higher than his Intelligence, this results in a bonus to these checks, while a lower Wisdom results in a penalty.

Hindrances

Unfortunately for the psychic, the pervading evil of Ravenloft taints most of the character's visions. Each time the psychic touches a psychically charged object, the most gruesome possible aspect of the object's past is revealed. If touching a dead body, the psychic should probably experience the very moment of the person's death. If a truly gruesome vision occurs, the psychic could make a fear or horror check (as determined by the Dungeon Master).

Entering sites where there has been (or will be, as dictated by the Dungeon Master and/or the adventure) *significant* terror of any sort requires an immediate madness check (modified as described previously). If the psychic is unaware that he has entered such an area, the check is made with an additional –4 penalty. However, if the hero indicates a conscious mental defense—a bracing up, so to speak—before entering such an area, a +4 bonus applies instead.

In addition, some magical items can affect a psychic's powers. A *ring of mind shielding* worn by a psychic obstructs the connection between the mind and the object touched, neutralizing the ability completely. Anyone else wearing such a ring does not emit readable psychic resonance. An *amulet of proof against detection and location* has the same effect.

REDEEMED

Basic Information

Classes Allowed:	Any
Races Allowed:	Any
Alignments Allowed:	Any Good
Ability Requirements:	Constitution 12+
	Wisdom 15+
Prime Requisite:	By Class
Starting Cash:	By Class x 1/2

Proficiencies

Available Categories:	Common
	By Class
	By Race
Bonus Proficiencies:	Religion
Recommended Proficiencies:	None

This kit is used for characters that were once evil but have since seen the light and become heroes. Redeemed characters may have been villains, henchmen, or just wayward souls, and they may or may not have failed a number of powers checks before finding their way back to the light. Any changes that she underwent during her darker days are assumed to have been reversed over the course of her redemption.

With the Dungeon Master's approval, this kit can be adopted in play by heroes who either undergo an alignment change, or who have failed one or more powers checks but manage to pull back from the darkness and ignore the siren call of evil.

Requirements

Redeemed characters can hail from any class or race, but they must be of good alignment. The whole premise for this kit is the struggle of a tortured soul to return to grace.

The rigors of this character's existence require her to be mentally and physically strong. As such, anyone created with the redeemed kit must have a Constitution score of not less than 12 and a Wisdom score of at least 15.

Description

There is no specific description associated with this kit. Even the most stalwart champions of good may have had dark moments in their past—a darkness that is deeper for some than for others. Although they can be of any class and race—Ravenloft natives or visitors from the jumble of worlds beyond the Misty Borders—all redeemed characters possess at least one unifying factor: Anyone

designed with this kit should carry some object that reminds her of her dark past. Whenever she is tempted to do evil again, she can look upon this item and strengthen her resolve in the matter.

Alternatively (or additionally), the character may carry an object that marks the start of her return to grace. This might be a holy symbol, a lock of hair from a loved one, or the weapon carried by a great avenger. Whatever it is, this object should be valuable above any other in the character's possession.

Roleplaying

Characters with the redeemed kit feel great guilt and shame for the things that they have done wrong in their lives. As such, they feel two very strong motivations.

The first is a desire to do all that they can to make the world a better place. Knowing firsthand the nature of darkness and evil, they are grimly determined to set right all that is wrong. They are haunted by the memories of the evil deeds they committed, and part of the character feels as though she can never fully atone for those deeds—but the next best thing is to actively combat evil in all its forms. These characters go out of their way to protect the innocent and go to great lengths to free peasants from the yolk of oppressors.

Of equal or even greater importance is their driving desire to set right the wrongs they committed in the past. If a redeemed character comes upon old associates who are still following the path of evil, or encounters a bad situation that she knows has arisen from some evil deed she herself committed, she sets aside all other business in an effort to make amends for her past evils. This could include dissuading her old comrades or bringing them to justice if that fails. In this respect, a redeemed character is as singlemindedly focused on doing good and defeating evil as is a paladin. In fact, folk tales in the Demiplane of Dread that revolve around holy warriors who ride out of the Mists to vanquish evil are, in fact, garbled accounts of redeemed ones trying to make amends for past evils.

Redeemed characters are often very religious. This is reflected in the bonus proficiency given to them, but it should also be visible in their actions during play. A redeemed character needs to be aware that she has been blessed with a second chance at life. When things go right, she should offer thanks. When evil threatens, she should ask for guidance and protection.

Benefits

Redeemed characters have seen the results of their own dark and evil sides, making them more able to resist its pull. Their ability to throw off such seductive influences gives them a willpower that most other characters can only strive to obtain. While this is primarily a roleplaying aspect, it has some game effects as well.

Whenever a redeemed character is called upon to make a saving throw that tests her willpower, she gains a +2 bonus. Examples of such saves include attempts to resist a *charm person* or *domination* spell. This bonus is cumulative with any modifier received for an exceptional Wisdom score.

Hindrances

The redeemed character must always battle the desire to use darker means to accomplish her goals. In her past life, evil and malevolence offered quick solutions to any problem. In fighting the good fight, however, the character must be constantly on guard.

A redeemed character cannot even tolerate evil acts on the part of companions. If she becomes aware that she is traveling in the company of someone who is committing evil deeds, the redeemed character must either force the individual to change his ways, somehow bring him to justice, or part company with him. If the redeemed character chooses the latter option, she will always feel compelled to atone for the evil she is allowing to continue. The potential trouble this can cause between party members is an outward display of the redeemed character's constant personal temptation to return to darker ways. (Optional rule: when a redeemed player character fails a powers check, she receives only the benefit of doing so, not the drawback, and she progresses two stages at a time.)

Redeemed characters cannot keep excess wealth. They may never possess more than ten magical items, and they must always donate a minimum of 10% of all treasure they gain to charities and other worthy causes.

Whenever a redeemed character is called upon to make a powers check, her chance of failure increases by half. Thus, an act that would have a 10% chance of failure for her peers increases to 15% for the redeemed character.

SPIRITUALIST

Basic Information

Classes Allowed:	Mage
Races Allowed:	Human
Alignments Allowed:	Any Good
Ability Requirements:	Intelligence 10+
	Wisdom 16+
Prime Requisite:	Intelligence
Starting Cash:	As Wizard

Proficiencies

Available Categories:	Common
	Wizard
	Human
Bonus Proficiency:	Spellcraft
Recommended Proficiency:	Religion
	Ancient History

Spiritualists are wizards who specialize in the calling, commanding, and combating of spirits, ghosts, and the incorporeal undead. Most of them use their skills to uncover the answers to ancient mysteries that only the dead and undead possess—such as the locations of hidden treasures, historical facts, or even the truth about existence beyond the current life. While the uninitiated may think of them as nothing more than necromancers by another name, there is much more to these mysterious folk.

Requirements

Because spiritualists are constantly under threat of enraging the spirits they deal with, thus becoming subject to ghost attacks, they spend much of their time studying the necromantic arts, hoping to unlock further secrets that will let them deal safely with these ghosts. For that reason, they must meet the same requirements as necromancers. A spiritualist must have an Intelligence score of at least 9 and a Wisdom score of no less than 16.

A spiritualist must be human, but he can be of any alignment. (Most demihumans in Ravenloft hold firm to the belief that the spirits and graves of the dead are not to be violated under *any* circumstances.)

Description

Spiritualists tend toward somber dress. They recognize that the magic they attempt to harness involves violating of the sanctity of the grave, which is not something to be taken lightly. Apart from that, however, one is as likely to find a spiritualist dressed in the dark robes of a wizard or rich silks of the gentry.

Roleplaying

A spiritualist is keenly aware that he treads a fine line between not only life and death, but also good and evil. To abuse the powers that have been given him is to risk absolute corruption and ultimate doom.

This attitude sets the spiritualist apart from the necromancer in a very distinct way. Necromancers deal primarily with the corporeal undead. They animate corpses and infuse skeletons with the essence of unlife. Their arts focus on the flesh once its animating spirit has been lost, and their goal, more often than not, is the accumulation of power.

The spiritualist, on the other hand, is interested in the reverse. He recognizes that the spirit is more important than the shell it wore in life. Where the necromancer forces the unliving flesh to obey his will, the spiritualist coaxes the dead spirits to do his bidding and lend him assistance.

Necromancers force undead into specific molds and functions that are dictated by the his specific outlook and needs, while spiritualists attempt to deal with the undead on their own terms. While this difference may seem minor in theory, it is very important in practice. As a whole, necromancers view the flesh and spirits of the dead as raw material that they can forge into weapons or tools. In contrast, the spiritualist views the flesh of the dead as an inviolate monument to the lives the spirits once led, and their minds as valuable sources of hidden wisdom; therefore, ghosts must be treated with the utmost respect.

Spiritualists often work closely with ghostwatchers, as the extraordinary talents of these individuals help them identify the location and nature of ghosts, thus making their search for knowledge easier. Another reason for the ability of spiritualists and ghostwatchers to work closely together is the fact that most spiritualists attempt to deal fairly with the ghosts with whom they interact. In exchange for the information or services they seek, they will often assist a ghost in achieving its final rest by taking steps to rectify the situation that has kept it trapped in this world. Ghostwatchers, who are often subjected to the intense emotional pain felt by ghosts, appreciate the efforts of the spiritualists when it comes to laying spirits to rest. Most often, they are glad to share their insight if it will ease the spirit's pain and suffering

While spiritualists try their best to honor agreements made with ghosts, there are lines many will not cross. Good-aligned spiritualists will endanger an innocent in the course of appeasing a ghost only under the most extreme circumstances;

spiritualist's opponents suffer a –1 penalty to their saving throws when attempting to resist his necromantic spells.

Spiritualists can cast the wizard spells *astral* spell, *past life*, and *trap the soul*, and the priest spells *speak with dead, restoration/energy drain,* and *undead ward* spells as if they were from the wizard's school of necromancy, provided they are of sufficient experience levels to cast such spells. (This means that the spiritualist's opponents also suffer a –1 penalty when saving against these spells.)

Beyond these benefits, however, spiritualists also have special skills when dealing with the incorporeal undead and the spirits of the dead. First, they receive a +2 bonus to all fear and horror checks involving incorporeal undead, as well as a +4 bonus to the saving throw to avoid the effects of a ghost's aging attack.

Hindrances

Due to their focus on the necromantic sphere of magic, spiritualists are unable to use spells from either the illusion/phantasm or enchantment/charm schools. In addition, they suffer a –15% penalty when trying to learn spells from schools other than that of necromancy.

Certain necromantic spells are anathema to the spiritualist because they violate his belief in the sanctity of grave and spirit. As such, no character created with this kit can learn or cast them. This prohibition applies to any spell that creates corporeal undead creatures (like *animate dead* or *Bloodstone's spectral steed*). Other spells that affect corpses exclusively, like *mask of death*, fall into this category as well. Dungeon Masters are free to rule that other spells are not available to spiritualists, depending upon their game effects.

Spiritualists who practice their craft in front of most natives of Ravenloft are often asking to be lynched. In a land where death and fear rule the night, a person who calls to the dead is considered evil, or at least possessed by dark forces. Therefore, spiritualists must take extreme care not to reveal their true natures to the general public. Any stranger insufficiently enlightened to understand that a spiritualist is not necessarily evil can be checked against the Encounter Reactions table (**Table 59** in the DUNGEON MASTER® *Guide*), using the "Threatening" column to gauge the reaction. If a "threatening" or "hostile" result comes up and the stranger has an opportunity to raise a mob, roll on the same table. Another "threatening" or "hostile" result means that a mob gathers. What happens then is up to the spiritualist and his friends.

evil spiritualists will hardly ever endanger a potential source of income or knowledge, likewise shielding innocents (and even many evil folk) from harm by ghosts. More often than not, spiritualists will even turn their talents to destroying thoroughly evil or insane ghosts, regardless of whatever deals they may have made in order to initiate such contact.

Finally, the spiritualists' frequent and extended dealings with the dead also impact their personalities. While they are somber when practicing their art, a fair number of spiritualists are quite hedonistic otherwise. The spiritualists deal with so many ghosts, who are consumed by regrets over things they failed to do while alive, that many take steps to avoid the same fate. Many others, however, carry the melancholy of death with them wherever they go.

Benefits

Their scrutiny of the dark arts grants the spiritualist a +1 bonus when making saving throws to resist spells of the wizard school of necromancy or the priestly necromantic sphere. In contrast, the

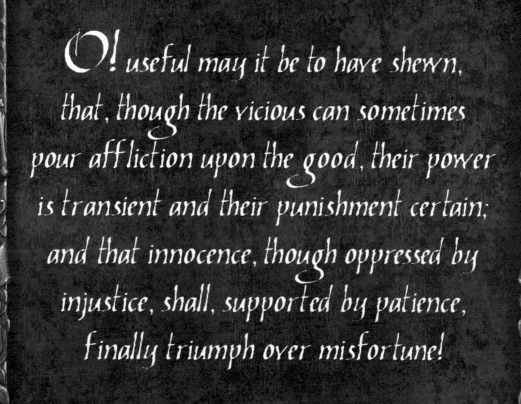

O! useful may it be to have shewn, that, though the vicious can sometimes pour affliction upon the good, their power is transient and their punishment certain; and that innocence, though oppressed by injustice, shall, supported by patience, finally triumph over misfortune!

—Ann Radcliffe
The Mysteries of Udolpho

Champions

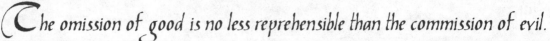

The omission of good is no less reprehensible than the commission of evil.

—Plutarch
Moralia (c. A.D. 100)

THE ENEMIES OF EVIL

The next several pages present the readers with detailed information on some of Ravenloft's greatest champions. Some of these have been drawn from game products while some others have come from the various novels set in the Land of the Mists.

Format

All of the characters presented in this section use a standard format. The following information is provided for each entry.

The Basics

Each entry begins with the character's name, followed by race and class. If the character has been designed using a kit, that appears in parentheses. Underneath this falls the character's alignment.

Complete game statistics follow this information. These include the character's ability scores, level, and combat information. A brief summary of any special attacks and defenses are included here, although these are more fully fleshed out in the text.

Summary

After the game statistics comes a brief summary of the character's place in the Demiplane. A quick perusal of this information should give the Dungeon Master a basic understanding of the character. Because it represents the common knowledge about the character, this text can also be used to provide information to characters that investigate the champion.

Appearance

A complete description of the hero's physical appearance comes next. This includes favorite clothes, heraldry, distinguishing features, and commonly carried equipment. Mentions of favored weapons appear in this section if they are especially noteworthy.

Background

This section provides a more detailed look at the character, giving information that should not normally be available to the heroes. Uncovering these facts should require either an extensive investigation on their part or an open conversation with the actual character. The latter may or may not be an option, of course, depending upon how tight-lipped that particular nonplayer character is.

Personality

The information presented in this section gives the Dungeon Master a feel for how to roleplay the character. In addition, it defines how the character is likely to act in certain situations. Unusual phobias or other mental traits appear in this section as well.

Combat

This section of the character's description presents complete details on the champion's favored weapons and strategies. In addition, any special attacks or defenses mentioned in the game statistics at the start of the entry are more fully described here.

Equipment

If the characters have any special items associated with them, these objects will be detailed in this section. In most cases, magical weapons, armor, and the like are discussed in the section on combat.

Adventure Hooks

The last part of each character description presents one or more ideas for adventures involving the character. Dungeon Masters can expand these, constructing brief encounters or even entire RAVENLOFT campaigns around them.

Further Reading

This section lists any other relevant products in which the character appears.

BROTHER DOMINIC

8th-Level Human Cleric (Guardian)
Neutral Good

Armor Class	9	Str	12
Movement	12	Dex	10
Level	8	Con	15
Hit Points	54	Int	15
THAC0	16	Wis	18
No. of Attacks	1	Cha	14
Damage/Attack	1d6 (quarterstaff)		
Special Attacks	Spells		
Special Defenses	Turn undead		
Magic Resistance	See below		

Brother Dominic is the head of one of Ravenloft's most interesting secret societies, the Order of the Guardians. The brothers and sisters of this monastic order search out dangerous magical artifacts and relics. Those items they can destroy are annihilated, but the others are hidden away, placed in secret shelters where their powers cannot endanger the outside world.

Appearance

Brother Dominic is a large man, with worn rugged features that show the hardship of his life clearly in every crease. His eyes are friendly and warm, showing the compassion and wisdom that mark him as a man of rare quality.

As a monk, Brother Dominic is most often draped in the heavy, gray robes of his order. These plain garments are adorned with only one thing: the holy symbol that he wore in his days as a priest. This is a symbol of a rising sun, worn on a thin leather cord. The circular brass amulet bears a simple disc with a curving line above it.

Background

Before joining the Order of the Guardians, Dominic served as a priest in his homeland. His insight and tenderness combined with a natural leadership ability to make him beloved of the faithful members of his order.

Unfortunately, these same things brought him into conflict with certain powerful members of the church hierarchy. Fearful that he would discover their own impiety and denounce them, they turned on Dominic and drove him out of his homeland. Fleeing the wrath of these powerful enemies, he entered the Mists and found himself transported to Markovia in the Demiplane of Dread.

Brother Dominic

Despite his success in his homeland, Dominic had always felt that there was an unfulfilled purpose in his life. Here, in the Land of the Mists, he discovered its nature. Dominic had the calling; he was destined to become a monk in the Order of the Guardians.

While in Markovia, he stumbled upon an isolated monastery. Over the course of the next several years, Dominic learned the ways of this monastic order. He also learned the lore of the *tapestry of dark souls*, a magical artifact that they kept locked away in that particular hidden shrine.

The tapestry, a relic of the Abber Nomads who roam the Nightmare Lands, had the power to ensnare evil beings. While this seemed at first to be a blessing, it was soon discovered that those without the calling could not look upon the tapestry without being affected by it. The instant that such folk set eyes upon the gray cloth, the evil within them magnified to diabolic proportions. The minutest envy would become a terrible jealousy, and a petty grievance could be augmented into a murderous desire for revenge.

Gradually, Brother Dominic rose through the ranks of the Guardians (as this particular order called itself) until he became its head. His greatest challenge came when Morgoth, the most powerful and evil being ever absorbed by the tapestry, escaped. Using his powerful magic and overpowering will, Morgoth assembled an army of undead and lycanthropes to attack the shrine of the Guardians. It was his desire to set free the other spirits in the tapestry and lead them in the conquest of Tepest and the destruction of the monks who had held him prisoner.

In the battle that followed, two of Morgoth's allies, one of them his own son, betrayed him. Their power, combined with that of the Guardians, proved too much for Morgoth. In the end, both he and the tapestry were destroyed.

This was the end of the Guardians as well. Without the tapestry to watch over and much of their shrine reduced to rubble by the battle, these monks went their separate ways. For a time, Dominic tried his hand at the vintner's art. The calling, however, was not so easily put to rest.

Dominic found himself pulled away from his new home by forces he could not resist. Stepping into the Mists, he emerged in the domain of Hazlik. There, he discovered a powerful artifact called the *Iron Flask of Tuerny the Merciless*. Recognizing the danger that this evil relic posed, especially if it should fall into the hands of Hazlan's wicked ruler, he claimed it for his own. Traveling into the wilderness of the southern Core, he established a small monastery similar to the one that had stood in Markovia. Thus, another branch of the Order of the Guardians was born. Because of the item it guarded, the wardens who lived there call this monastery the Iron Sanctum.

Personality

Dominic takes the responsibilities he has assumed very seriously. He allows nothing to violate the sanctity of his order or endanger the deadly treasure that they protect. The weight of this burden combines with his many years to make him appear somber and pensive at times.

Despite his somewhat stoic appearance, however, Dominic is a kind and compassionate man. He considers himself a defender of the weak and protector of the innocent. He generally comes to the aid of others, unless his duty to the order mandates otherwise.

Combat

Dominic is a pacifist at heart. Still, he recognizes that the road he has chosen is a perilous one indeed. He has been called upon to engage in battle before and knows that he will do so again.

When traveling or anticipating the need to defend himself, Dominic relies upon a stout quarterstaff. This is shod with silver on one end and cold iron on the other, making it effective against a variety of creatures like lycanthropes and some types of fiends.

Although Dominic still has his priestly powers, he seldom uses them. If he has the time to prepare for an encounter, he may be ready to employ spells. (See "Spell List" below.) As long as he has his holy symbol with him, Dominic is also able to turn undead.

Dominic has a natural immunity to magical spells from the wizard's school of enchantment/charm and the priest's charm sphere. In game terms, this functions as 40% magic resistance. This resistance applies not only to magical abilities but also to psionic powers that mimic the aforementioned spells. Other powers may or may not be affected, as determined by the Dungeon Master. He may freely waive his resistance to a spell or power at any given time.

Dominic knows a great deal about the history and lore associated with Ravenloft's most infamous and dangerous artifacts. This knowledge is reflected in a skill similar to the bard's ability to "know a little bit of everything." In his case, however, it applies to only magical objects, artifacts, and relics. In game terms, this gives him a 40% chance of recognizing a magical artifact when he sees it.

Due to the vows he took upon joining the Order of the Guardians, Dominic may possess one suit of magical armor, one magical shield, no more than four magical weapons, and a maximum of only four other items. As he seldom adventures, this has never proven to be a problem for him.

Dominic is also required to tithe 10% of any income to the order. Again, however, this seldom comes into play.

Spell List (5/5/4/3): 1st—*bless, combine, command, create water, cure light wounds, detect evil, detect magic, detect poison, detect snares & pits, endure cold, invisibility to undead, light, locate animals or plants, magical stone, protection from evil, purify food & drink, sanctuary, shillelagh, remove fear.*

2nd—*aid, augury, barkskin, chant, detect charm, dust devil, enthrall, find traps, fire trap, flame blade, heat metal, hold person, know alignment, produce flame, resist fire, sanctify, silence 15' radius, slow poison, speak with animals, spiritual hammer, withdraw, wyvern watch.*

3rd—*animate dead, continual light, create food & water, cure blindness or deafness, cure disease, dispel magic, feign death, flame walk, glyph of warding, line of protection, locate object, magical vestment, meld into stone, negative plane protection, prayer, protection from fire, pyrotechnics, remove curse, remove paralysis, speak with dead, starshine, stone shape, summon insects, water breathing, water walk.*

4th—*abjure, animal summoning, call woodland beings, cloak of bravery, cure serious wounds, detect lie, divination, free action, imbue with spell ability, neutralize poison, protection from evil 10' radius, protection from lightning, reflecting pool, spell immunity, tongues.*

Equipment

Apart from his quarterstaff, the only piece of equipment that Dominic regularly carries is his bronze holy symbol. In addition to its use in spellcasting, this object is magical. By speaking a brief prayer, he can cause the symbol to glow with the light of day (as a *continual light* spell) until he dispels it.

Adventure Hooks

Brother Dominic is an excellent patron for any group of adventurers. As such, an entire campaign

can be built around the Order of the Guardians. Such a scenario would feature the heroes as members or agents of this order. Their exploits would center on attempts to recover magical artifacts of great power and even greater evil. Once secured, these would be returned to their sanctuary and secured in its hidden catacombs.

Two excellent sources on magical items for which the heroes could be searching are the AD&D *Book of Artifacts* and the four-volume *Encyclopedia Magica*. A third source would be *Forged of Darkness*, which features an assortment of magical items found only in the RAVENLOFT campaign setting.

It seems likely that Dominic's order may soon find themselves coming into conflict with Hazlik, the evil sorcerer who rules over the domain of Hazlan. He knows that the *Iron Flask* has been seen in his realm and has some understanding of its diabolical power. Although the wards of the Guardians have kept him from learning about their order or the treasure they hold, it is only a matter of time before this changes. When that happens, the Guardians will need all the allies they can find.

Dominic can be used to introduce the guardian kit to the group if one of the player characters is interested in taking it, or if the Dungeon Master wishes to present the opportunity for the heroes to join during the course of an adventure. Dominic might be getting on in years and looking for someone to replace him, or he might be recruiting for the order. He can openly declare his intentions to find a worthy hero who will join in his sacred duties, or he can surreptitiously observe the adventuring group and subtly test the various members. If when and the time is right, Dominic could offer the player character the honor of joining the Order of the Guardians. If his offer is accepted, he will reveal the secrets of the order. (The player can study and employ the kit presented earlier in this book, and the Dungeon Master can privately impart any relevant secrets pertaining to the campaign.) As soon the player character discovers a dangerous item—especially one sought by evil forces—and swears to protect it from discovery, she becomes a guardian and officially adopts the kit.

Further Reading

The story of Brother Dominic's original monastery and the item that it guarded appears in the RAVENLOFT novel *Tapestry of Dark Souls*. In addition, the RAVENLOFT module *Neither Man Nor Beast* details another branch of the Order of the Guardians.

DRAGONOV, IVAN

20th-Level Human Ranger (Monster Hunter)
Chaotic Good

Armor Class	9 (4)*	Str	18/00
Movement	12 (15)*	Dex	15
Level	20	Con	17
Hit Points	139	Int	10 (4)*
THAC0	1 (13)*	Wis	14
No. of Attacks	2 (3)*	Cha	9
Damage/Attack	1d10+6 (1d4/1d4/2d4)*		
Special Attacks	Surprise, spells, +3 to attack rolls in human form due to Strength		
Special Defenses	Hit only by gold weapons or those of +1 or better enchantment (when in loup-garou form), regeneration		
Magic Resistance	40%		

*Dragonov's abilities vary based upon his form. The parenthetical numbers apply to his lycanthrope form.

Ivan Dragonov is both one of Ravenloft's greatest heroes and perhaps its greatest tragedy. He is a monster hunter who has become what he most hated. Afflicted with the dread disease of lycanthropy, Dragonov uses these bestial powers in his endless war against the creatures with whom he is now kindred.

Appearance

Ivan Dragonov is a powerfully built man whose massive frame makes him look even more imposing and dangerous than many of the monsters he hunts. His features are rugged and worn, grim and foreboding.

Dragonov's hair is fiery red, hanging down to his shoulders. A full beard of slightly darker crimson hangs from his ruddy cheeks. The dark tan on his arms is broken only by a lattice of white scars, remnants of countless battles against the minions of the night.

Background

Ivan Dragonov is a native of Stangengrad, which is in the domain of Falkovnia. He has hunted monsters, and lycanthropes in particular, since coming of age. In all those years, only one monster has managed to elude him, the monstrous Adam of Lamordia. Although this failure upsets the resolute Dragonov, he has not allowed himself to become obsessed with that single instance.

As a child, his size and strength made him something of a bully. He seemed to be headed for the life of a thug until he met a priest named Hamer. This man offered soothing words and wise counsel to the child. In the end, he persuaded Dragonov to use his physical might in the fight against evil and the protection of the innocent.

Dragonov pursued his chosen profession with a singleminded devotion few have matched. He studied the arts of combat, making up for his size and relative slowness with a brutality and ferocity that few enemies could equal. Knowing that his career would require him to travel and stalk his prey through the wilds of Ravenloft, he also studied the lore of the forest. No monster would ever escape him because he lacked provisions or shelter.

Shortly after he embarked on his career as a monster hunter, Dragonov had an encounter that changed his life. He was called in to assist in capturing a beast that had been slaughtering the farm animals near Stangengrad. When the giant rat was snared, it proved to be a local youth afflicted with the dread disease lycanthropy. With the aid of the priest Hamer, an effort was made to cure the boy. As his mother watched, however, Hamer's spells failed and the boy reverted to his bestial form. Knowing that there was nothing else to do, Dragonov stepped forward and killed the lad.

The suffering of that poor family moved Dragonov greatly. The fact that an innocent boy and his loving mother could be made to withstand such torment convinced him that there was no evil in the world worse than that of lycanthropy. From that day on, he swore that he would seek out these creatures of the night above all others.

Years later, another event changed Dragonov's life again. While battling a loup-garou, he himself was infected with lycanthropy. Though the beast within him subsequently helped to save the young woman Hilda Kreutzer from the evil monster Adam, he was doubtful as to whether he could control this power.

His suspicions were confirmed when he fell in love with a beautiful redhead named Gabrielle. When she confessed her love to him, the emotions that overcame him began to trigger his transformation. Before he could get away, however, he realized that she too had undergone a change; she had become a giant spider and was trying to kill him!

After destroying the monster his beloved had become, Dragonov decided that his lycanthrope status could not be trusted. He went to his mentor,

Hamer, and asked him to either cure his condition or kill him with his own silver weapon. However, when the cure failed and Dragonov transformed, the silver weapon proved ineffective. Ivan regained consciousness to find himself standing over his dead friend's body.

He then realized that his curse would not be so easily thwarted. He decided to use the powers of the beast in hunting the creatures that had made him what he was.

From the day he killed Hamer, Dragonov aged no more. He has wandered the Demiplane of Dread for nearly two hundred years now, hunting lycanthropes and trying to atone for Hamer's murder. Even though he has long since discovered a cure for lycanthropy, he refuses to use it on himself until he has tracked down and killed each and every loup-garou in Ravenloft.

Personality

When he is not actively stalking a beast, the mighty Dragonov devotes much of his time to physical exercise and training. He does not drink anything stronger than tea to keep his flesh and spirit pure. He refuses fancy meals and other refinements that, in his opinion, make men soft and susceptible to the influences of evil.

Dragonov is a religious man, but his relationship with the gods is a curious one. Primarily, this is due to the fact that he has not yet decided if he is battling for or against their wishes. He has seen so much evil in the world that it is difficult for him to accept the fact that the powers who rule the world are not themselves evil.

Although a practical man, Dragonov can be very singleminded. He is not prone to compromise, since he sees the world in absolutes: There is good and there is evil. If you are not one, you are the other. This philosophy has served him well in his life, although it has caused him problems in his dealings with people like Victor Mordenheim. While he has allied himself with Mordenheim on more than one occasion to battle Adam, Dragonov considers the doctor hardly better than the abomination he created.

Due to the bloodlust that overcomes him in his loup-garou form, Dragonov is constantly on guard for any situation that could force his transformation. When not hunting a beast, he tries to maintain control of his temper. He fears the berserker rage that could cause him to harm innocent people. This inner struggle causes him to appear tense and uncomfortable around most people.

Ivan Dragonov

Combat

Whenever Dragonov becomes extremely emotional or angry, his lycanthropy is triggered. As such, whenever he enters battle, he is inevitably in a bestial state. This transformation takes one round. While in loup-garou form, he flies into a rage that is terrible to behold. He will attack and attempt to slay anyone nearby, regardless of whether it is prospective prey or an erstwhile ally.

If he is in his wolf form, Dragonov's keen senses impose a –2 penalty to his enemies' surprise rolls.

As a loup-garou, Dragonov is a dangerous enemy. His savage bite inflicts 2d4 points of damage, and each of his claws can strike for 1d4 points.

Though he did not know this when he gave his friend Hamer the silver sword to slay him, Dragonov is actually a mountain loup-garou. Thus, only gold weapons or those of +1 or better magical nature can harm him when in lycanthrope form. Magical weapons that are not made of gold can inflict no more damage than their magical "plus." Thus, a steel *dagger +2* can inflict a maximum of 2 points of damage per strike. Gold weapons without a magical "plus" inflict only a single point of damage per hit.

His supernaturally boosted physiology gives Dragonov a 40% magic resistance. This bonus applies whether he is in his normal or man-wolf form. In addition, Dragonov regenerates one hit point per turn.

As a ranger, Dragonov has a number of special abilities. These include his skill at surviving in the wilderness as well as a natural ability to track prey (with a +6 bonus). He can hide in shadows with a 99% chance of success and move silently with an equal chance of success.

Because he favors a two-handed weapon (his great axe), he seldom takes advantage of the ranger's ability to use two weapons at one. The same is true of the ranger's normal archery bonus, which is negated by his use of a crossbow.

The bestial blood that flows in Dragonov's veins is anathema to all natural creatures. As such, he has lost the animal empathy ability natural to all ranger characters, and he has never gathered any animal followers.

Dragonov knows far more about the habits and lore of lycanthropes than the average adventurer. In any given situation, he has a feeling for what the monster will do. This experience provides him with a +2 bonus on any proficiency or ability check made in the course of stalking these creatures within a turn of its passing. In combat, this knowledge is helpful as well. Whenever he attacks a lycanthrope, he gains a +2 bonus on all damage rolls.

Unfortunately for him, his enemies have begun studying him as well. This is reflected in a +2 bonus that lycanthropes gain to their initiative rolls in any combat against Dragonov.

Dragonov has managed to master some spellcasting, but he is uncomfortable in its use.

Spell List (3/3/3): 1st—*animal friendship, entangle, invisibility to animals, locate animals or plants, pass without trace, shillelagh.*

2nd—*barkskin, charm person or mammal, goodberry, messenger, snake charm, speak with animals, trip, warp wood.*

3rd—*hold animal, plant growth, snare, spike growth, summon insects, tree.*

Equipment

Although he seldom has to do battle when not in his loup-garou form, Dragonov always likes to have a weapon at hand, just in case. As a rule, he carries a massive double-bladed axe (which inflicts 1d10 points of damage). This weapon has a silver blade,

making it especially effective against lycanthropes. He also carries a heavy crossbow.

In addition to this, Dragonov seems to collect strange equipment, especially those things recommended by the late Rudolph van Richten for hunting werebeasts. As for weapons, he carries a bronze knife, an oak cudgel, an iron dagger, a copper short sword, and a quarrel of miscellaneous arrows tipped with silver, coral, bone, flint, and obsidian. Dragonov also carries many other substances to aid in his fight against werebeasts. He usually has at least some wolfsbane (with which he is *very* careful), poppy seeds, belladonna, camphor, acid, and several extra oil flasks.

Adventure Hooks

A group of player characters could encounter Ivan Dragonov during virtually any adventure in which they are hunting a monster. This is especially true if their prey happens to be a lycanthrope.

Conversely, the heroes could find that the monster they have been hunting is none other than Dragonov, while he himself is on the trail of a dangerous enemy. The adventurers might join forces with Dragonov before they learn his true nature.

Ivan Dragonov has vowed to return to Lamordia one day and settle his score with both the monster Adam and his creator, Victor Mordenheim, who both seemed to have survived the passing of time. This quest could well bring him into contact with any heroes who are also investigating that accursed pair.

Another angle from which to approach Dragonov is in the role of the hunted . . . by superior forces. A group of ultra-lawful adventurers, considerably higher in level than the player characters and bent upon the destruction of Dragonov, causes the loup-garou to beg for help. His pleas are especially effective if he and the heroes have the same goals, and Dragonov could even be the key to their quest. Having to protect a lycanthrope is a challenge on several levels in the Demiplane of Dread, one that can be incorporated into the ongoing campaign or be treated as an individual adventure. Depending on who hunts for him, Dragonov's tendency to turn into a violent beast might be the least of the party's problems.

Further Reading

Ivan Dragonov also appears in the RAVENLOFT novel *Mordenheim* and in the short story "The Vanished Ones" in the *Tales of Ravenloft* collection.

GONDEGAL

**15th-Level Human Avenger
(Knight of the Shadows)
Chaotic Good**

Armor Class	3	Str	17
Movement	12	Dex	14
Level	15	Con	16
Hit Points	120	Int	14
THAC0	6	Wis	15
No. of Attacks	2	Cha	15*
Damage/Attack	1d8+4 or 1d8+6 vs. shape changers (magical sword, Strength, specialization)		
Special Attacks	Spells, +2 to attack rolls due to Strength and specialization		
Special Defenses	Bonus hit points		
Magic Resistance	Nil		

*This becomes 16 when dealing with Falkovnians, who are under his protection. However, it becomes 14 when dealing with residents of neighboring domains.

At one time the conqueror of Arabel, on the distant world of Faerûn, Gondegal has always lived by the sword. After entering the Mists, he lived for a time in Falkovnia, a brutal land well suited to his mercenary nature. In time, however, the truth about that domain and the rest of this strange land became clear to him.

Appearance

Gondegal is a large, muscular man who stands well over six feet in height. His long gray hair is usually worn loose, and he sports a long moustache that droops down to below his jaw.

Gondegal almost always wears a suit of black plate armor. Emblazoned on the breastplate is a red-eyed, gray wolf's head, the ancestral mark of his family. He wears a black and yellow cape, as do all of Ravenloft's Knights of the Shadow, secured by a clasp bearing an eclipsed sun.

When he walks, the so-called Lost King has a confident, almost arrogant, stride. He radiates the self-assurance of a long-time campaigner whose mettle has been tested against more enemies than he can remember. If ever there were a natural born leader of men, it is Gondegal.

Background

Gondegal's story begins on the world of Faerûn, in the Forgotten Realms. In the year 1352 DR

(Dalereckoning), Gondegal and a force of mercenaries took the city of Arabel. It was his intent to carve out his own kingdom, making his court in that place.

Although a valiant warrior and a masterful general, Gondegal was not much of a king. In short order, his early victories were swept away by the combined armies of Sembia, Cormyr, Tilverton, and several of the Dalelands. He had made powerful enemies by his actions, and his army was no match for such an alliance.

After the armies of Cormyr liberated Arabel, Gondegal vanished into the wilds. It was—and generally still is—believed by those in the area that he became a bandit king. Stories of the "Lost King" and his cadre of fanatically loyal followers persist in the form of tales about caravan raids and other such actions.

In truth, however, Gondegal's fate was very different. His flight from the armies of Cormyr carried him farther than even he could have planned. Moving into an area of foggy marsh to escape his pursuers, Gondegal found himself swallowed up by the Mists of Ravenloft. He

Gondegal

eventually emerged in the domain of Falkovnia.

At first, Gondegal was intrigued by the militaristic nature of life under the iron hand of Vlad Drakov. While he did not approve of the atrocities committed by Falkovnia's monarch, he was himself an experienced general and understood the need to keep order in the ranks.

In time, however, Gondegal began to understand that there was more to this land than he had at first seen. The stink of evil that filled Falkovnia began to choke him.

Gondegal was slow to act, however. He recognized that his failure on Faerûn was due in part to the haste with which he had acted. As they say in Arabel to this day, "Gondegal's reach was longer than his blade." This time, he was determined to be seen not as a conqueror, but as a liberator. He would take control of Falkovnia and, this time, the populace would rally around him.

Sadly, Gondegal's campaign failed. Although he escaped capture, his allies and organization were crushed before they could even begin their coup. Once again, however, defeat changed Gondegal's life.

In escaping from the armies of Falkovnia, Gondegal fled into neighboring Necropolis (then Darkon). He hope to find sanctuary there, knowing that he had entered a land which had often battled the armies of Vlad Drakov. Long before he could seek out the ruler of that nation, however, a trio of vampires attacked him.

Despite his skill and the power of his magical sword, Gondegal fell before these terrible creatures. As they began to sup on his life force, the Lost King slipped into darkness, certain that his life had come to an end.

The Mists, however, had decreed otherwise. Gondegal awoke several days later. He was badly wounded and being nursed back to health by the squire of a powerful knight. This warrior, who gave her name as Helna Vladinova, was a member of the Circle, an organization composed of Ravenloft's Knights of the Shadows.

In the months it took him to convalesce, Gondegal spoke at length with the woman who had saved him. By the time he was well enough to leave her care, he had decided that his life had gone astray. He began to realize that there was important work to be done in Ravenloft, and that people like Helna were doing it. Thus it was that he decided to join the Circle and become a Knight of the Shadows.

In the years since that time, Gondegal has grown in wisdom and gradually began to recover the experience levels that he lost to the vampire attack. He has taken the plight of the Falkovnians to heart, and made their welfare the focus of his life. As a Knight of the Shadows, he vows not to give up his war against Vlad Drakov until one or the other of them is destroyed.

Gondegal's dedication to his new order has won him the respect and admiration of his peers. In 751 he underwent the ceremony of Final Ascension to become the head of that order. Gondegal, the Lost King, is now far more than the bandit prince that the people of Arabel once believed him to be.

Personality

The Lost King draws a great deal of inner strength from the fact that he has at last found a calling in life. His dedication to the Circle is absolute, a fact that can be seen in his change of alignment. (He was chaotic neutral when he first wandered into Ravenloft.) Nothing can force Gondegal to willingly shirk his duty.

He has also taken a liking to the idea of being a hero. In the past, he was respected and admired by his followers and feared by his enemies and the common folk. Now, while his allies and enemies have not changed their opinions of him, the average citizen of Falkovnia is quick to praise his efforts on their behalf. Thus, Gondegal is known to the populace of Falkovnia as the defender of the oppressed and ally of the weak. His reputation earns him a +1 bonus to his Charisma score when dealing with the citizens of that domain. Outside the realm, however, the same confidence and self assurance makes him seem arrogant and domineering. Thus, when dealing with folk in nearby realms he suffers a –1 penalty to his Charisma.

Gondegal's fondness for adventure has not slackened with his membership in the Circle. He still favors a fight to any posturing or diplomacy. His choice of enemies has changed, however, and he attacks only those who have earned his wrath. Gondegal has also learned something new in his time as a Knight of the Shadows. He has discovered mercy, a concept utterly alien to the warrior who once tried to force his rulership on the people of Arabel.

Combat

In combat, Gondegal depends upon *Scourge*, his magical blade. *Scourge* is a *long sword +1, +3 vs. lycanthropes and shape changers*. He has found this to be a most valuable blade in his pursuit of ultimate justice.

In addition, Gondegal's status as an avenger has allowed him to specialize in the use of the long sword. This gives him a +1 bonus on his attack rolls and a +2 bonus on his damage rolls. These, combined with his natural Strength bonus of +1 to both attack and damage rolls, make him a very deadly enemy.

Gondegal wears the plate armor associated with his order but almost never employs a shield or other defensive item. He has been known to employ magical defenses, but only in rare circumstances.

When facing any foe that reminds him of his enemy, Vlad Drakov, Gondegal receives 5 bonus hit points due to his determination and avenger's drive. If facing Vlad Drakov himself, this increases to 10 bonus hit points. Any damage he takes is removed from these temporary hit points before he himself is wounded in any way.

Gondegal has spent a great deal of time studying the methods and means by which Drakov's men maintain their version of law and order. As such, he has an innate understanding of their probable action in any given situation. When he is stalking such enemies, a successful Wisdom check indicates that he has a "gut feeling" about where his enemy has gone or what he will do.

As a Knight of the Shadows, Gondegal can also cast spells as a paladin. However, he still cannot turn undead, and his opponents receive a +1 bonus to their saving throws against his spells.

Spell List (3/2/1/1): 1st—*cure light wounds, detect magic, detect poison, detect snares & pits, endure cold, locate animals or plants, magical stone, protection from evil, sanctuary, shillelagh.*

2nd—*augury, barkskin, chant, detect charm, find traps, know alignment, resist fire, slow poison, speak with animals, spiritual hammer, withdraw.*

3rd—*dispel magic, line of protection, locate object, magical vestment, negative plane protection, prayer, protection from fire, remove curse, remove paralysis, speak with dead.*

4th—*cure serious wounds, detect lie, divination, protection from evil 10' radius, protection from lightning, reflecting pool, repel insects, spell immunity, tongues.*

Equipment

Gondegal carries *Scourge*, his magical long sword. He wears special black plate mail and the yellow cape that marks his order.

Adventure Hooks

Gondegal and his fellow knights are brave warriors, each devoted to protecting the citizens of a given region. For his part, the Lost King keeps his watch in the domain of Falkovnia.

Characters who run afoul of the lord and law in that accursed domain might find Gondegal a valuable ally. He can be introduced to almost any adventure in which the heroes are in need of a hand while traveling in the realm of Vlad Drakov.

In addition, Gondegal's determination to see brutes like Vlad Drakov torn from power makes it very possible for him to act as a patron for one or more adventures. He might hire the characters to create a diversion while he himself undertakes some other mission. Or, if the heroes have shown themselves to be heroes of honor and valor, he might ask them to actually join him in a raid on Drakov's palace.

If any character in the party is also a Knight of the Shadows, Gondegal can take on the role of a mentor. As the leader of the Circle, he could call upon such characters to undertake any number of missions. Because of the way in which the Circle operates, however, he is slow to order a knight away from the lands he protects.

Perhaps the most interesting adventure that might be set around Gondegal involves his annual pilgrimage to the domain of Avonleigh in the Shadowborn Cluster. The player characters might be called upon to travel with him, especially if one or more of their number is also a Knight of the Shadows. Conversely, the heroes might be tasked to see to some work that must be done in Gondegal's absence.

A third variation on this theme might see them hired by agents of Vlad Drakov to follow and destroy the Knight of Falkovnia. This possibility is an excellent way for heroes unfamiliar with Gondegal to meet him. At first, they may see him as an enemy, but eventually they would learn the truth about him and he might even become a valuable ally.

HERMOS

0-Level Human
Neutral Good

Armor Class	10	Str	18
Movement	12	Dex	9
Level	0	Con	15
Hit Points	6	Int	10
THAC0	20	Wis	13
No. of Attacks	1 (fists)	Cha	12
Damage/Attack	1d2+2 (Strength bonus)		
Special Attacks	+1 bonus on attack rolls		
Special Defenses	Nil		
Magic Resistance	Nil		

Hermos the man-giant serves as both foreman and spiritual leader for Carnival, a festival of the macabre that wanders the Demiplane of Dread. This huge man manages the band of outcasts for the mysterious master of the freakshow, Isolde. He also gathers information for her about the domains through which they travel. In his own quiet way, Hermos has transformed the term "freak" into a badge of honor for misfits throughout Ravenloft.

Appearance

Hermos stands almost ten feet tall, but his long, awkward limbs still manage to look out of proportion for his narrow body. He dresses in very plain clothing, marked only by the small silver pendant he wears on a chain around his neck. This pendant bears the imprint of a hare with long knotted ears—Tidhare, the Ear-Tied Hare.

The man-giant always wears an expression of serene kindness. Even those frightened by his great size are usually calmed when they catch sight of his gentle face.

Background

Hermos was born Francis Ciantioux in the city of l'Morai. From an early age, he began to compare himself to the Ear-Tied Hare. According to the local children's stories, this rabbit suffered and died because of the other animals' pride and anger. Francis empathized with the hare, as he himself suffered much abuse from his drunken parents, Phillipe and Margorie Ciantioux.

After Francis hid from his angry parents one too many times, his father called the gendarmes to find the boy. Under the strict laws of l'Morai, Francis was convicted of disobedience.

As punishment, the Councilors decreed that the boy would be transformed into a man-giant so that he would never be able to hide again. Thus, "Hermos the Amazing Man-Giant" was created and taken to live in Carnival l'Morai with the other freaks. Because of the magic used to transform him, Hermos remembered nothing of his former life.

After several difficult years, he befriended the blind juggler, Marie, when she discovered a murdered performer in her wagon. As she and Hermos investigated the incident, they began to uncover the dark secrets of the carnival and its evil Puppetmaster. First, they discovered that the murder she had witnessed was merely one in a long series of slaughters. It seemed that someone had been killing off the freaks for quite a while.

Even more importantly, they discovered that they and the other performers had not always been freaks. These misfits had all been sentenced to the carnival for breaking the Statutes of l'Morai, and they were all marked with small red tattoos on the backs of their necks—tattoos that marked them as freaks.

Marie, Hermos, and the other accursed entertainers planned a rebellion against the Puppetmaster and the townsfolk who had created them. Still, they were no match for the l'Morai armies, who surrounded the carnival and laid siege. Despite Hermos's protests, Marie surrendered herself to the Councilors to save the other performers.

When she returned, however, a great change had overtaken her. As their general, Marie ordered the freaks to abandon the fight and rebuild the site. Though they were confused, the performers began to follow her orders. Hermos, however, was not so easily fooled. He knew that his friend would never before have wanted them to return to their former lives. Thus, when he saw that she wore the symbol of the Puppetmaster, he immediately recognized that she had become the new carnival master.

To rescue the surviving freaks, Hermos embraced Marie one final time, breaking the blind juggler's neck and saving her from a terrible future. He announced to the others that Marie had ordered them all to flee. Immediately, all the remaining performers ran from l'Morai and escaped into the Mists.

In honor of Marie's sacrifice, Hermos never revealed his friend's final secret to anyone. He told the other freaks that she remained behind to prevent the Puppetmaster from following after them. Thus, Marie became a martyr as well as a hero to these cursed performers.

When the ragged fugitives emerged from the Mists, they stood in the domain of Darkon. At a loss for what else to do, the freaks began to do what they knew best: perform. For a while they traveled around, putting on shows in exchange for money and supplies. However, the residents often treated them badly, often refusing to pay or even running them out of town.

Undaunted, the performers left Darkon. The next domain they traveled to, however, was even worse. The lord sent his soldiers to round up the freaks and bring them to his palace to "entertain" him. As the freaks were being "escorted" to the palace in chains, a beautiful woman appeared and single-handedly defeated the soldiers, who could not seem to harm her with their clumsy weapons.

Viewing her as their savior, the freaks just assumed that Isolde would travel with them, and she did. In fact, some of the fugitives even believed that their brave, blind general sent her to save them.

Though this mysterious woman now provides protection for the entertainers and transports them from place to place, she always refuses her share of the profits. Hermos is the only person around whom she seems to be comfortable, and she leaves most of the responsibility of running Carnival to him.

Personality

Hermos is an extremely quiet individual. He rarely speaks to anyone when not conveying Isolde's orders or preaching. He is never happier than when he is talking about Qin-sah, God of Horses, and Tidhare, God of Freaks.

Instead of making him bitter and cynical, the atrocities he suffered in l'Morai have left him generous and thoughtful. Hermos is always willing to help others, and has inspired a great deal of devotion and cooperation in the members of Carnival.

Combat

Hermos is not much of a fighter, but he will defend himself if threatened. Most often, he depends on his great size and strength to intimidate people, preventing them from harassing him.

Equipment

Hermos rarely leaves Carnival, so his wagon is usually nearby. Thus, he does not carry much equipment with him. However, he always wears a pendant engraved with the image of the Ear-Tied Hare.

Adventure Hooks

Carnival could appear seemingly overnight on the outskirts of a town the heroes are currently in. If so, one (or several) of the townsfolk might approach the heroes and try to convince them that the carnival is populated by evil, dark-hearted beings—their twisted physical forms representing the dark nature of their spirits. They would then hire the party to capture Carnival's evil ringleader, the man-giant known as Hermos. If the characters investigate, however, they should discover the true, good-aligned nature of Hermos.

Another option arises if the heroes have recently confronted a domain lord and are being pursued by his minions. Just as the heroes are cornered and almost overwhelmed by their foes, a number of freaks leap from nowhere to their aid. Hermos arrives on the scene and offers them security in Carnival. The domain lord will almost certainly attempt to place other minions between the heroes and the safety of Isolde's strange, traveling festival. In fact, his minions may even pursue them beyond the borders.

Traveling with Hermos and Carnival should be a strange and uncomfortable experience for the player characters, not a refreshing respite from the evil of the domains and their denizens. Certainly the freaks of Carnival do not pose a direct threat to the heroes, but little is as it seems in this traveling show, and the unwary might get hurt or be subjected to fear, horror, and madness checks. Some of the freaks live in conditions that are dangerous to most people (like the poison-eater, the pinman, and especially the clowns), while others are horrifying to look upon when they remove their masks or hoods. There are fairly knowledgeable folk in the domains who claim it is *unhealthy* to remain in Carnival for long, though reports of what that means vary wildly from one source to another.

Isolde, for all her hospitality, is not sociable, and Hermos himself will prevent visitors from attempting to approach her. He may even become violent if anyone attempts to force the issue. No matter how friendly the man-giant and the heroes become, he will never betray Isolde, and he will never divulge the secrets of Carnival (mostly because he does not even know what many of them are).

Further Reading

The story of Carnival l'Morai is told in the RAVENLOFT novel *Carnival of Fear*. In addition, Carnival and Isolde appear in Chapter Five: Secret Societies in *Domains of Dread*.

KOLYANA, TARA

5th-Level Human Anchorite
Lawful Good

Armor Class	10	Str	8
Movement	12	Dex	14
Level	5	Con	13
Hit Points	30	Int	15
THAC0	18	Wis	17
No. of Attacks	1	Cha	15
Damage/Attack	1d6 (quarterstaff)		
Special Attacks	Spells		
Special Defenses	Turn undead		
Magic Resistance	Nil		

Tara Kolyana has always been an idealistic and somewhat naive young woman. Her natural kindness and mercy brought her into the Church of Ezra, where she found the peace and contentment of faith.

While most anchorites are hermits or monks, she has traveled the lands of the Core trying to heal the sick and bring comfort to the suffering. Her good efforts have won her the appellation *fille des anges* (fee-yuh deh zanj) or *daughter of the angels*.

Appearance

Tara is a beautiful woman. Her emerald green eyes are always bright and friendly, the perfect accent to her creamy complexion and sunset-red hair. Her full lips are seldom seen to frown, and the gentle curve of her cheeks gives her the countenance of the angels she is said to have been raised by.

In her travels, Tara shuns wearing any armor. She depends upon her faith and the blessings of Ezra to protect her from harm. Instead, she favors simple robes, usually green in color. She adorns these with her holy symbol, an icon depicting the alabaster shield and slender sword of Ezra.

Background

Tara was born in the domain of Barovia in the year 718. When she was still an infant, her parents carried her out of that domain and took up residence in Hazlan.

As a child, Tara was always known for her temper and emotions. She was quick to anger, passionate in her beliefs, and adamant in her compassion for the weak and defenseless. She was something of a tomboy and a thrill seeker, never satisfied with life in the small farming village to which her parents had moved her.

Tara's life underwent a major change when she was a teenager. A great wolf was plaguing the farmers and shepherds of her village each night. While the villagers laid traps to kill the beast, Tara felt this was inhumane. After all, the wolf was merely trying to survive. In an effort to save the beast's life, she built a sturdy cage, baited it, and waited. The next morning, she found that her trap had snared not a wolf but a naked man.

It was obvious to everyone that the man was a werewolf, suffering from the effects of lycanthropy. Luckily, the village priest was able to cure him with the help of a Vistani troupe that was passing through town.

After this first brush with the supernatural, Tara became acutely aware of the many dangers that stalked the mists. She began to travel, trying to find the best way to help out others that had fallen victim to the dark hand of fate. After a few years or so of adventuring, she found her calling and joined the Church of Ezra. Since that time, she has advanced in the priesthood as an anchorite and earned the respect of all those she comes into contact with.

Personality

Tara has changed much in the intervening years. She has found an inner peace that is reflected in her every action. No longer is she a child of emotion, driven by passions as dangerous to herself as to others. She has found her place in the world and is content to spread the blessings of her faith to those in need. She retains her composure even in the most dangerous situations.

Tara is very much a pacifist. She refuses to take the life of any intelligent creature. Enemies who are defeated need only be subdued for a time, in her opinion, not slain. The daughter of angels is also quick to come to the aid of the wounded. After any battle, she does what she can for both friend and foe alike.

Luckily for her, she has fewer qualms about battling the walking dead. She believes the undead to be suffering under a terrible curse. In her mind, destroying such monsters allows their spirits to rest peacefully.

Equipment

Tara seldom carries much equipment with her. Beyond her green robes, she generally travels only with her quarterstaff, holy symbol, prayer book, and rations.

The holy symbol that she wears displays the alabaster shield and sword of her faith. It has been enchanted so that it functions as a 9th-level *amulet versus undead*.

Combat

As mentioned above, Tara is a pacifist. She sees no point in violence and attempts to withdraw from or avoid any such encounters. She uses force only in defense, and even then only when no other option presents itself.

Tara has the normal ability of clerics to turn undead creatures away. In addition, she carries an *amulet versus undead* which can do the same. Although the latter is more powerful than she, Tara always attempts to use her own turning ability before relying on her amulet.

In times of need, usually when she is attempting to avoid an enemy, Tara has the ability to seek safe haven in any temple dedicated to the worship of Ezra. The exact interpretation of "safe haven" varies depending upon the similarity of Tara's alignment to that of the temple clergy. At the very least, however, she can expect to be fed and clothed, her wounds tended to, and her presence within the temple kept secret.

As a lawful good anchorite, Tara has the ability to cast priest spells. Tara never employs spells that cause physical harm to an enemy (except the undead). Thus, she never uses reversed cure spells or the like.

Spell List (5/5/2): 1st—*bless, combine, command, cure light wounds, detect evil, detect magic, detect poison, detect snares & pits, endure cold, light, locate animals or plants, protection from evil, purify food & drink, remove fear, sanctuary.*

2nd—*augury, barkskin, detect charm, enthrall, find traps, hold person, know alignment, resist fire, sanctify, silence 15' radius, slow poison, speak with animals, withdraw, wyvern watch.*

3rd—*continual light, dispel magic, glyph of warding, line of protection, locate object, magical vestment, negative plane protection, protection from fire, remove curse, remove paralysis, speak with dead, starshine.*

Adventure Hooks

When the player characters encounter Tara, she is almost certainly on some kind of mercy mission. Whether this involves healing the injured, curing the sick, or trying to redeem some villain will vary depending on when and where they encounter her.

Tara Kolyana

Tara can be found whenever the heroes have dealings with the Church of Ezra. Although she is not well placed in the church hierarchy, her popularity has won her more than her rightful share of influence. Of course, this has also garnered her some powerful enemies within the church itself.

As a representative of the clergy, Tara can act as a go between whenever the heroes are dealing with the Church of Ezra or other anchorites. She might intercede on their behalf if they are in need of the church's resources or even recommend them for some mission.

Tara's pacifistic nature and strict code of personal ethics can make her a frustrating traveling companion. This is especially true in the case of warriors, who generally believe that the answer to any problem can be found at the tip of a sword.

KREUTZER, HILDA AND FRIEDRICH

2nd-Level Human Mages (Spiritualists)
Lawful Good

Armor Class	10	Str	8/10*
Movement	12	Dex	12/11*
Level	2	Con	10/9*
Hit Points	6/5*	Int	16/15*
THAC0	20	Wis	17/16*
No. of Attacks	1	Cha	12/14*
Damage/Attack	1d8** (snaplock pistol)		
Special Attacks	Spells		
Special Defenses	Nil		
Magic Resistance	Nil		

*Statistics are for Hilda/Friedrich.
**On a roll of 8, roll again and add the damage.

Hilda and Friedrich live in the domain of Necropolis, in the city of Martira Bay. They have a basic training in the dark arts, but neither has a particular interest in pursuing such things anymore. Instead, they depend upon their writing to earn them a living. Although they shun adventuring, it has a way of forcing itself upon them—something that neither of them has ever grown very comfortable with.

Appearance

As a couple, Hilda and Friedrich complement each other well. While she is taller, he is more physically attractive. Where she is more decisive, he has the heart of a poet. Both are in their middle twenties.

Hilda's appearance can best be described as somewhat mousy. Although rather plain looking, however, she is not unattractive. Her build is tall and slender, without any natural tendency toward athletics or other physical pursuits. She wears her burnished copper hair short, in a style probably better suited to a man than a woman. Her brown eyes are keen and alert, sparkling with intelligence and curiosity.

Friedrich is a handsome man whose pampered upbringing shows plainly in his bright smile and light build. His hair is a crown of golden curls which tumble just below his collar and complements his ruddy complexion well. He has bright, compassionate blue eyes and a charming smile that has led many adventurers to dub him as nothing more than a pretty boy.

Background

Friedrich and Hilda met while spending time in a graveyard in search of inspiration for their writings. For a brief time, they were both students of an aged arcanist named Herman von Schrek in Il Aluk, Darkon. After the death of their mentor, they were hired by Victor Mordenheim to assist in his attempts to restore his beloved Elise to life.

During their stay at Schloss Mordenheim, the golem darklord Adam kidnapped Hilda. Bound and gagged, the beast carried her to the Isle of Agony in the Sea of Sorrows. In an effort to rescue her, Friedrich joined with Mordenheim and the monster hunter Ivan Dragonov. Together, they set out across the ice floes to the Isle of Agony.

In the meantime, Hilda had come to know Adam fairly well. Even though she was his prisoner, she saw in him a tortured spirit who, even if he were evil, was not the monster that Mordenheim had made him out to be. In short, Hilda and Adam became friends of a sort.

The trio of men arrived on the Isle of Agony and found Hilda while Adam was off hunting. When he returned to find his prisoner missing, the monster flew into an enraged pursuit. Overtaking them on the ice floes, he attacked. Dragonov moved to defend Hilda, Friedrich, and Mordenheim. Much to everyone's surprise, the great warrior transformed into a vicious beast, battling Adam for all he was worth. In the end, both Dragonov and Adam fell through the ice into the Sea of Sorrows. Leaving the combatants for dead, the others returned to Schloss Mordenheim.

Once there, Mordenheim demanded that they continue their work toward reviving his beloved Elise. His plan was to place the spirit of his wife in the body of a young Vistana woman named Ilise. Ilise's spirit would be lost in the process, but that meant nothing to the mad doctor.

Hilda refused, her experiences with Adam having convinced her that Mordenheim was the true monster. With the aid of Adam, who had actually survived the frigid waters of the Sea of Sorrows, they thwarted Mordenheim's plans.

As they were fleeing Lamordia, Hilda tried to cast a spell to aid in their flight. When she did so, the Mists swirled in around them, making the path impossible to navigate.

For several hours, the couple stumbled around in the Mists. When they finally emerged in the domain of Darkon, they immediately knew something was wrong. They continued on their way, stopping in the first village they encountered.

Hilda and Friedrich

After talking to the innkeeper about their strange encounter, they began to piece together what had happened to them. Somehow, they had been transported almost 175 years into the future!

Convinced that the dark arts themselves were to blame for their experience, the couple vowed to refrain from using magic in the future. However, they soon realized that many people could be helped by their skills. They eventually came to the agreement that they would use magic only to help those in need.

They still had the money they had earned in Lamordia, so Hilda and Friedrich eventually bought a small house outside of the capital. Luckily, they were researching a minor mystery for a friend in Martira Bay when the city of Il Aluk was destroyed. Having no place else to go in the world, they took up residence where they were and returned to their literary pursuits.

They have recently heard tales of a great monster hunter named Dragonov, but they are quite sure it is not the same man who defended them in Lamordia so many years ago.

Personality

The Kreutzers are reluctant adventurers at best. They are more likely to undertake a journey in search of inspiration for her prose or his poetry. Still, they are reluctant to refuse an honest entreaty from someone in dire need of their knowledge of necromancy and metaphysics.

Of the two, Hilda is by far the more practical. It is she who handles their money and any business matters that arise. While Hilda is certainly not unfeeling, she is far more realistic than Friedrich. She thinks of her husband as something of a dreamer and a romantic.

Friedrich is a good deal more expressive than his wife in many ways. His gregarious nature more than compensates for her cooler personality, making the two a popular couple at social affairs. As might be expected, Friedrich has a poet's outlook on the world. He tries to find the feelings and emotions in everything.

Combat

Neither Hilda nor Friedrich is especially skilled in combat. As such, they do all that they can to avoid it. While both are very brave, neither has any misgiving about turning and running when trouble arises.

If they are going into a situation in which they suspect danger, they generally arm themselves with snaplock pistols. In times when battle seems certain, they often enlist the aid of a few reliable warriors.

Although both Hilda and Friedrich have an understanding of spiritualism and magic, neither is comfortable enough with these powers to make much use of them in combat. They know that there are many hazards associated with the magic of the dead, even when it is used for good, and they do not wish to take unnecessary chances.

Still, their knowledge of magic does give them the normal advantages associated with spiritualists. The Kreutzers receive a +2 bonus to all fear and horror checks involving incorporeal undead, as well as a +4 bonus to the saving throw to avoid the effects of a ghost's aging attack.

Further, they gain a +1 bonus when making saving throws to resist spells of necromancy while their targets suffer a –1 penalty to their saving throws. Both Hilda and Friedrich gain a +15% bonus on their chance to learn any necromantic spell. Lastly, any new spells they create that fall into the school of necromancy are researched as one level lower.

The Kreutzers are unable to use spells from either the illusion/phantasm or enchantment/charm schools. In addition, they suffer a –15% penalty when trying to learn spells from schools other than necromancy. Neither of them can learn or cast spells that involve the creation of the corporeal undead.

Spell List (2): 1st—*affect normal fires, alarm, burning hands, chill touch, comprehend languages, dancing lights, detect magic, detect undead, erase, feather fall, identify, light, magic missile, message, unseen servant, wall of fog, wizard mark.*

Adventure Hooks

The Kreutzers' informal role as paranormal investigators who often hire bodyguards makes them ideal patrons for any adventure set in Martira Bay. The heroes could either seek information or help from the Kreutzers in particularly strange cases or be hired by the couple to protect them while they solve a case.

An excellent adventure could be built around the kidnapping of Hilda by agents in the employ of Mordenheim. Despite the time that has passed, the doctor has not forgotten their role in thwarting his plans. He hopes to make them help him transplant the brain of his cursed wife into a living body. It is his plan to use Hilda's body, thus avenging himself for her betrayal of him in the past.

The adventure begins with the heroes being hired by Friedrich to join him in his mission to rescue his wife. Over the course of the journey, Mordenheim's agents also take Friedrich. If the heroes are to rescue him, they must seek out Adam and convince him to come to their aid.

With Adam's help, the heroes return to Schloss Mordenheim and confront the doctor. After overcoming a number of perils drawn from his dark science, they rescue the couple and dispatch, at least for a time, the master of Lamordia.

The Kreutzers are also on good terms with the Vistani. They could easily be of help to heroes who need to contact these gypsies of the Mists. There are, after all, few giorgios who have an open invitation to travel with the Canjar tribe (especially the Zsolty family).

As mentioned earlier, the Kreutzers are a couple removed from their own time by almost two centuries. That premise can become the basis for an extended campaign wherein they seek help from the player characters to return to their own time. Possible quest hooks include the following:

- A search for the Manusa tribe of Vistani, who understand the ebb and flow of time better than anyone else in the Demiplane. They can provide the means to return the Kreutzers to their own time, or they can at least enigmatically point the way. (See *Van Richten's Guide to the Vistani* for information on the Manusa.)
- A search for a time portal in the Mists, as well as the key to open it, which may or may not be found with the help of the Vistani.
- A slow descent into madness for either Fredrich or Hilda, or both, until a solution is found. Losing all they knew and called home just proves too much for them to take.
- Mordenheim may have learned that the Kreutzers, who helped to thwart his plans to destroy Adam and regain his wife, have reappeared in the domain, and he can send agents to exact his revenge.

Further Reading

Friedrich and Hilda Kreutzer also appear in the RAVENLOFT novel *Mordenheim*.

RAY, ALANIK

10th-Level Elf Thief
Lawful Neutral

Armor Class	7	Str	8
Movement	12	Dex	17
Level	10	Con	9
Hit Points	38	Int	17
THAC0	16	Wis	17
No. of Attacks	1	Cha	13
Damage/Attack	1d4+4 (*dagger +4*)		
Special Attacks	Backstab (x4); +1 to attack rolls with straight bows, short swords, and long swords		
Special Defenses	90% immune to *sleep* and *charm* spells		
Magic Resistance	Nil		
Thief's Skills	Pick Pockets (45%)		
	Open Locks (65%)		
	Find/Remove Traps (45%)		
	Move Silently (75%)		
	Hide in Shadows (70%)		
	Detect Noise (60%)		
	Climb Walls (80%)		
	Read Languages (80%)		

Often called simply "the Great Detective," Alanik Ray was born to a family of elf nobles in the city of Neblus in Necropolis. At a very young age he began to notice that not everyone enjoyed the privileges that he did. All around him, his keen mind saw corruption and deceit. When he came of age, the young elf turned his matchless intellect upon the criminals and wrongdoers of society.

Appearance

Alanik Ray is very slender, even among the lithe elves. He stands just over six feet tall but weighs only one hundred pounds. His features are sharp and angular, with keen eyes set beneath a knife-edged brow.

The great detective's long hair is golden in color. He wears it drawn back, giving him a pronounced widow's peak and what appears to be an unnaturally high forehead.

Alanik Ray is seldom found in anything less elegant than silk or satin. His favorite outfits are generally golden with ornate red and blue embroidery. Despite their light, flowing appearance, all of Alanik's outfits have numerous pockets and the like sewn into them. Here, he conceals the tools of his trade, *Goldenfang* (his favored weapon), and the occasional pistol.

Background

Alanik Ray's parents were well placed in the upper class of Neblus. His father, Ardal Ray, was purported to be a skilled merchant and cunning businessman. As he grew to manhood, Alanik Ray enjoyed all the benefits of his father's station. However, it did not take long for him to notice that others were not so well off. He took to leaving behind the trappings of his father's manor and exploring the neighborhoods of the common folk. In these dismal places, he saw crime and corruption at every turn.

Even more surprising to the young Alanik was the discovery that his father was a major dealer in the black market and narcotics trade. He confronted his father with these accusations and soon found himself disowned.

Over the course of the next year, Alanik Ray learned whom he could and could not trust in the city watch. He gradually became the greatest nemesis of crime in the city of Neblus. When Alanik saw his father's criminal holdings broken up, his ties to the past were finally and irrevocably severed. To further distance himself from these events, the young detective left Neblus and made his way to Mordentshire.

Despite the prejudices the locals have against demihumans, Alanik Ray soon built himself a reputation based on his skills as a detective. Thanks to large fees paid for his services by wealthy clients, he has become wealthy himself.

During this time, he met and befriended Arthur Sedgwick, a young physician. The two became close friends and began to work together on the cases that were brought to Alanik Ray. On more than one occasion, Sedgwick's medical knowledge has saved the Great Detective's life.

A few years ago, Alanik Ray accepted an offer to assume control of the constabulary in Martira Bay. Unfortunately, his obsession with justice led the Kargat to view him as quite a threat. Thus, upon Azalin's disappearance, they took the opportunity to try to rid themselves of the Great Detective. Alanik barely escaped with his life, relocating to Port-a-Lucine, where his friend Arthur joined him.

Arthur has recently committed some of Alanik's adventures to paper in his well-received volumes *The Life of Alanik Ray* and *The Casebook of Alanik Ray*.

Personality

Alanik Ray is a man with a passion for mystery and deduction. He has a special interest in those cases that show either an especially cunning villain or have an air of the supernatural about them.

The Great Detective grew up in the lap of luxury, and he never lost his taste for the finer things. He dresses in the finest clothes, drinks only the best wines, and otherwise pampers himself at all times. Many have wrongly dismissed him as a whimsical fop upon their first meeting.

Alanik has inherited his father's business skills as well. He charges his wealthy clients as much as the market will bear for his services. When someone without such resources brings him a particularly interesting case, however, he is quick to undertake the matter without a fee. His expenses, he knows, can be made up the next time someone with deeper pockets comes to call.

Combat

Alanik is 90% immune to all *sleep* and *charm* spells. He also gains a +2 bonus on madness horror checks. As an elf, he also gains a +1 attack bonus when employing any straight bow, short sword, or long sword. As a thief, Alanik also has a 75% chance to use magical scrolls.

Due to his ability to move silently, Alanik imposes a –4 penalty on his opponent's surprise rolls. If he must open a door or other portal to reach the foe, this penalty reduces to –2.

As payment for one of his earlier investigations, Alanik Ray was presented with a magical dagger. This weapon, named *Goldenfang*, has been his pride ever since. *Goldenfang* is a very slender *dagger +4* that is cast from what appears to be solid gold.

From time to time, Alanik Ray feels the need to arm himself more heavily. At those times, he typically carries a wheellock pistol, which inflicts 1d8 points of damage.

Equipment

The Master Detective carries with him a great assortment of equipment, all designed to help him in his investigations. The most well known of these are his ever-present magnifying glass, an assortment of lockpicks, and a notebook in which he seems to record every detail of every case.

Alanik Ray also has a few magical items that he brings to his investigations. Chief among these are a monocle that functions as *eyes of minute seeing* and a *hat of disguise,* which he uses for covert studies.

Alanik uses a number of powders, tinctures, and chemicals in his work. These are often mistakenly assumed to be magical by those who do not understand the science behind them.

Adventure Hooks

Most likely, any adventure involving Alanik Ray will be something of a criminal investigation. This does not, however, mean that there cannot be an element of the supernatural in the case as well.

Uppermost in Alanik Ray's mind is the mysterious disappearance of Rudolph van Richten, the famous authority on the supernatural. While the two men had not seen one another for several years, both had a keen interest in the other's affairs. If the characters have played the events in the module *Bleak House* (in which case they have met the Great Detective), they can provide information to close out Alanik's investigations.

Also of interest to the Great Detective is the strange crime lord whose power seems to be growing in Port-a-Lucine. Although he does not know the nature of this man, he has been convinced that the matter may well merit his attention. What Alanik does not understand, however, is that his would-be adversary is not human, but the living brain of Rudolph von Aubrecker (see the *RAVENLOFT MONSTROUS COMPENDIUM® Appendices I & II*). An investigation in this matter almost certainly brings the heroes to the attention of not only the living brain but also the darklord of Dementlieu and his minions: the Obedient.

Yet another way to use Alanik Ray in a campaign is to make him an employer for the adventuring party. The detective accepts any case that interests him, but this occasionally results in overbooking. Ray is a great believer in researching, and many of his cases cannot be solved without accumulating a great deal of background information. Still, he does not necessarily feel that he has to do the legwork personally. Therefore, he might attempt to hire a party of rough-and-ready assistants to discover the truth of certain reports or retrieve objects that are relevant to his caseload. For example, he might send them to determine if a haunting is real or a hoax, or he might need them to track down a murder weapon in another domain. In this capacity Ray is all business, and he can send adventurers in search of virtually anything without explaining why he does so. Only if some member of the party showed excellent deductive skills would he consider discussing his cases, which would make the adventurer something of a partner, at least for the present job.

SNOWMANE, LARISSA

6th-Level Human Druid
Neutral Good

Armor Class	6	Str	12
Movement	12	Dex	18
Level	6	Con	15
Hit Points	38	Int	13
THAC0	18	Wis	17
No. of Attacks	1	Cha	18
Damage/Attack	1d3 + poison (whip)		
Special Attacks	Spells		
Special Defenses	Spells, *dance of the dead*		
Magic Resistance	Nil		

Larissa Snowmane is the owner and captain of the showboat *River Dancer*. She has explored all of the Core domains as well as visiting countless Islands of Terror and Clusters. She is, without a doubt, one of the most well-traveled citizens of the Mists.

At heart, Larissa is an entertainer, although she was never what one would consider a bard. In recent years, however, the raw magical talents within her have begun to awaken. With the help of the Maiden of Souragne and the lord of that sweltering domain, she has become a powerful spellcaster.

Appearance

Larissa is a woman of astonishing natural beauty and exceptional charisma. This enchanting dancer has an exceedingly fair complexion and ice-blue eyes. Her most noteworthy feature is the pale white hair. These ice-hued locks were the reason she took the stage name "Snowmane."

Larissa's lithe form is well muscled and statuesque, although she moves with the almost unnatural grace of a trained acrobat. Her every movement, even the slightest gesture, is agile and flowing.

When not in costume, Larissa favors the elegant clothing of the gentry. She knows that her attire has a great deal to do with how others perceive her, and as captain of the *River Dancer*, she always tries to appear both professional and elegant.

If she knows that she is going to be called upon to use her magic, however, Larissa's garb is far less sophisticated. Knowing that nothing can be allowed to restrict her dance in any way, she wears only those clothes demanded by modesty. For the same reason, she always wears her hair loose and flowing, never bound.

Background

Larissa Snowmane was the only daughter of a man named Aubrey Helson. When he lost a large sum of money to the captain of a showboat, her father was killed and the little girl claimed as payment for the debt. Thus it was that she came to be the ward of her so-called "Uncle," Captain Raoul Dumont of the enchanted paddleboat La *Demoiselle du Musarde*.

From an early age, Larissa's unique and stunning looks combined with her natural agility and grace to make her a splendid dancer. As she grew up, never aware of her uncle's dark nature, she became one of the star entertainers aboard that magical showboat. As La *Demoiselle* plied the rivers of the Core, she saw countless ports in countless lands.

Not long after Larissa's twentieth birthday, Dumont piloted his ship through the Mists and, ultimately, into the domain of Souragne. While in this domain, she learned that her uncle was actually a slaver. In a hidden hold of La *Demoiselle*, he imprisoned a small menagerie of magical creatures. Through mystical means, he tapped the powers of these tortured folk to augment the natural abilities of his beloved ship.

In addition, Larissa discovered Dumont had struck a devil's bargain with the necromancer Alondrin (or Lond, as he preferred to be called). In exchange for passage out of Souragne, Lond would replace the crew of La *Demoiselle* with zombies, able to do their work without tiring or pay. One by one, Dumont and Lond began to murder the crew, animating their bodies and blaming the whole affair on a mysterious "swamp fever."

With the help of her lover Willen, Larissa fled into the dark swamps of Souragne. In those steaming depths, Larissa met the mystical Maiden of the Swamp. The Maiden helped her to remember an important event in her past, one that changed her life forever: When Larissa was only five years old, she was chosen by the swamp spirits, who drew her into the murky woods. There, she encountered the *feu follets*, who changed the hue of her hair and left her with the mark of the swamp's favor, making her a "Whitemane" and giving her the gift of dance.

The Maiden taught her how to harness this natural magical power within her, transforming her from a mere dancer to a powerful druid. With her newfound powers and the help of the Maiden's creatures of the swamp, Larissa planned to return to La *Demoiselle* and see justice served.

Before this could happen, however, Larissa would have to go before Anton Misroi, the lord of Souragne. Though the Maiden trained Larissa only

Larissa Snowmane

in "fruit and flower" magic, Anton taught her one bit of "blood and bone" magic. He saw the power within her and augmented these abilities by showing her the magical *dance of the dead*. Basking in the glow of her newfound magic, Larissa failed to fully understand the danger associated with that spell.

The battle that followed was terrible indeed. Dumont's harnessed sorcery and Lond's army of zombies fought the assembled forces of the swamp and Larissa's newly mastered magic. In the end, the beautiful entertainer decided the matter with the *dance of the dead*. Her victory was hollow, however, for Willen had seen her magical dance. While this evil power may have enabled the forces of the swamp to triumph, it slew all those, friend and foe alike, who witnessed its use. Dumont and Lond were dead, but so was her beloved Willen.

Freed of Dumont's hand, the crew of *La Demoiselle* drafted Larissa as their new captain. She renamed the paddleboat *River Dancer* and set about making amends for the wrongs committed by its former owner. In the years since that time, she has become one of Ravenloft's most well-traveled and knowledgeable adventurers.

Personality

Larissa has a natural affinity for the magic of the natural world, a gift that shows in her personality. She cannot stand to see any creature in physical pain or mental anguish. Her compassion and warmth extends to intelligent creatures as well as the beasts of the jungle and even the mysterious monsters in the Mists. During her travels, Larissa often finds herself coming to the aid of those in distress.

She keeps her own quarters fairly austere, for her enjoyment comes from magic, nature, and dancing. This is not to say that she shuns the comforts and pleasures of the physical world, only that they have little intrinsic value to her.

Combat

Larissa is loath to enter combat, generally trying to avoid battle whenever possible. When forced to do so, however, she uses her magical control over the elemental forces of nature to great effect. The unusual nature of Larissa's dance magic is reflected in the fact that all of her spells have only a somatic component. This is balanced by a 50% increase in the casting time of all her spells.

In the most extreme of circumstances, Larissa may choose to perform the *dance of the dead*. One round after she begins (unless she is somehow interrupted), she creates an invisible barrier around her with a fifty-yard radius. No mindless undead creature can enter the area of effect; self-willed undead must make a successful saving throw vs. spell to enter the area. Any undead creature already within the area cannot move (per the *hold undead* spell). Living beings caught within the fifty-yard radius must make a successful saving throw vs. spell or look upon this horrifying dance and immediately perish. Anyone who dies in this manner becomes a zombie under Larissa's control. If the rules from the *Requiem* box are being used, the Dungeon Master may allow player characters slain by this spell to continue play as undead heroes.

If she opts to enter melee instead of using her spells, she employs an unusual magical weapon given to her by Anton Misroi. Outside of combat, this weapon appears to be nothing more than a leather riding crop. In battle, however, it lengthens to become a lashing viper. Each round, she may strike with this whiplike weapon for 1d3 points of damage. Anyone hit by it must make a successful saving throw vs. poison or die instantly from the bite of this viper lash. Because this item was the gift of Anton Misroi, it requires powers check every time it is used.

Larissa can also identify plants and animals with perfect accuracy, pass through overgrown areas without leaving a trail, and gains a +2 bonus on all saving throws against fire or electrical attacks. However, she does not have the ability to turn undead.

Spell List (5/5/3): 1st—*animal friendship, bless, combine, create water, cure light wounds, detect evil, detect magic, detect poison, detect snares & pits, entangle, faerie fire, invisibility to animals, locate animals or plants, pass without trace, purify food & drink, shillelagh.*

2nd—*augury, barkskin, charm person or mammal, detect charm, dust devil, find traps, fire trap, flame blade, goodberry, heat metal, know alignment, messenger, obscurement, produce flame, sanctify, slow poison, snake charm, speak with animals, trip, warp wood.*

3rd—*call lightning, flame walk, hold animal, locate object, meld into stone, plant growth, protection from fire, pyrotechnics, snare, speak with dead, spike growth, stone shape, summon insects, tree, water breathing, water walk.*

Equipment

Larissa's most valuable possession is her magical paddleboat, the *River Dancer*. On this conveyance, she and her company travel the rivers of Ravenloft. This elaborate boat is nearly two hundred feet long and roughly fifty feet wide. It has a clean white hull with a bright red paddle wheel in the stern and a golden griffin for a figurehead. Its four decks are terraced affairs looking rather like the layers of a cake. A great calliope stands near the stern, filling the air with festive music and bursts of colored steam as the ship makes its way into port.

Cached aboard the *River Dancer* are a variety of magical items. These are primarily trinkets used to augment the entertainments offered by the ship's company. Larissa most commonly employs a silver, emerald, and jet pendant that looks very much like an eye. When the pendant is held in a closed fist (thus covering the "eye"), the wearer is affected as by an *invisibility* spell.

Adventure Hooks

Larissa's travels in Ravenloft make her an easy character to introduce to any campaign. Indeed, a whole campaign could be established around a group of heroes who have found employment on the *River Dancer*.

In addition to her travels, Larissa's accumulated knowledge of the Core and other realms makes her a valuable ally and source of information. Characters who need to know what they will encounter when they enter a domain that is new to them find Larissa a veritable font of useful knowledge.

An interesting adventure involving Larissa and the crew of the *River Dancer* might involve a return to Souragne. She has not returned to that place since the death of her uncle. She knows that there is much she can learn from the Maiden, but she is very reluctant to return there. Although she does not admit it, even to herself, this is due to a fear of Anton Misroi—as well as a feeling of affinity for the zombie master and his power.

Knowing all too well the hazards of the swamp, Larissa could hire the characters as additional guards for the dangerous passage through the Mists. Once in Souragne, it might become apparent that Misroi has decided to keep Larissa with him this time, instead of allowing her to leave. Since the *River Dancer* represents their best hope of escape from the swamps, the heroes must oppose this. Finding a way to defeat Misroi likely proves next to impossible, leaving the heroes with little choice but to strike some sort of bargain with the lord. While his demands should be tailored to the talents of the party, one can be certain that they will certainly not be palatable.

Bards have additional opportunities in an adventure involving Larissa and *River Dancer*. They can win passage for the entire party by promising to perform each night in exchange for passage. Players who enjoy roleplaying their characters could be asked to audition for Larissa before she allows the group to come aboard. If the hero performs well, the rest of the group will be taken aboard as guests of the captain. If the hero performs badly, she will use him for comic relief, but the other members of the party may have to cook, clean, or otherwise earn their passage. In either case, the bard becomes a member of the *River Dancer* cast, which offers a number of possible adventure hooks:

- One of the crew is a wererat who, during the show, attacks a person wandering the along the misty wharf at every port-of-call.
- One of the cast, a favorite performer of Larissa's, develops a fatal attraction for one of the heroes.
- Someone is replacing stage props with deadly replicas, causing mutilation and death in the midst of several performances.

Further Reading

Larissa Snowmane also appears in the RAVENLOFT novel *Dance of the Dead*.

WEATHERMAY, GEORGE

12th-Level Human Fighter
Neutral

Armor Class	8	Str	16
Movement	12	Dex	16
Level	12	Con	14
Hit Points	81	Int	13
THAC0	9*	Wis	18
No. of Attacks	3/2	Cha	8
Damage/Attack	1d8+3 (*long sword +2* plus Strength)		
Special Attacks	Nil		
Special Defenses	Nil		
Magic Resistance	Nil		

*Because he fights with two weapons, Weathermay receives a –1/–3 penalty on his two attack rolls. These penalties were somewhat offset by his Dexterity bonus.

George Weathermay is to the common people of Ravenloft what the late Rudolph van Richten was to the scholars of the Demiplane. However, his fame is not for his great insight into the nature and motivations of evil creatures but instead for his talent at destroying them.

Known simply as "Weathermay" in the many tales told of him throughout the Core, he was born of a wealthy family in Mordent. However, he has all but abandoned this heritage to pursue the evil spirits and other creatures that haunt the Land of the Mists.

Appearance

Weathermay is a tall, lean man with slender, hawklike features and dark brown hair slightly streaked with gray. His eyes are dark and seem to cut straight into a person's soul. His face is mostly expressionless, but when faced with a particularly challenging mystery or foe, his brow furrows in concentration and his thin lips draw taut. He tends to dress completely in black, favoring broad-brimmed hats that keep both the rain and sun out of his eyes, and large, billowing cloaks that make it hard for opponents to gauge whether or not he is armed until it is too late.

He rides a coal-black warhorse, which some tales describe as a nightmare. In truth it is simply well-trained and very aggressive.

Background

The Weathermay family is said to be one of the wealthiest in all of Ravenloft. Their assets include virtually all of the land in the domain of Mordent as well as Heather House, the most elegant manor in that realm. There are many rumors swirling around the Weathermays in regard to how they came by their wealth. The darkest of these imply that one of the family's progenitors struck a bargain with a "creature" who then cursed the land.

Born in 709, George Weathermay decided at an early age that he was going to clear his family's name. Though he was a gentle boy who would have wanted nothing more than to enjoy the peacefulness of nature, he devoted himself to studying the sport of hunting and the art of war. His parents could tell their son disliked these activities, but they could not dissuade him from his course.

As he matured, it became clear that the lad was never going to be comfortable in the presence of his peers. Indeed, he was distinctly uneasy with any group of people. Despite—or perhaps because of—this handicap, Weathermay had a great affinity for animals. Horse and hound, cat and chipmunk, all seemed to feel no fear in the presence of this mild tempered boy.

In time, Weathermay became a warrior of modest skill. Finally, at the age of seventeen, he left his comfortable home for a life of adventure and danger. His goal was to destroy evil wherever he found it and to make the Weathermay name synonymous with heroism rather than treachery.

As the years passed, Weathermay discovered (and destroyed) evils both supernatural and common. Indeed, Weathermay's fondest wish eventually came to pass: The stories of his heroism caused the blight on his family name to fade. Men and women all across the Demiplane came to associate his name with a mighty champion of justice. Alone, and in the company of some of the Demiplane's greatest warriors, he had defeated villains ranging from petty, tyrannical bullies to insane liches. He even joined Dr. Van Richten on a couple adventures, and although the two men had greatly different outlooks on how to deal with evil, they gained a deep respect for each other.

Although he spent most of his time traveling, he still visited his ancestral home every now and again, specifically to spend time with his young twin nieces Gennifer and Laurie Weathermay-Foxgrove, whom he loved as though they were his own children. For years, they were the only human beings to whom he was close, as his quest to destroy evil in all its forms filled the rest of his life.

In 741, it seemed as though this might change. Weathermay met a gorgeous, exotic-looking woman named Natalia. Though he turned into a stuttering, nerve-wracked fool around other women, he felt perfectly at ease around her. After a whirlwind, passionate romance, they vowed to marry. However, when he took her back to meet his parents in Mordent, she turned out to be a werewolf bent on revenge against Weathermay's friend Rudolph van Richten. Natalia was just using the great warrior to get close to the scholar without alerting him. In the ensuing battle, one of Weatherman's beloved nieces, Gennifer, was gravely injured. (They were visiting Van Richten in his shop when Natalia attacked.) The girl would have died if not for the doctor's swift and expert medical attention. Meanwhile, Natalia escaped, vowing to return for another attempt at taking Van Richten's life.

It was a grim Weathermay who headed north from Mordent, looking for clues about the identity of Natalia. His determination eventually led him to the Vhorishkova family in southeastern Verbrek. None there would help him locate Natalia, and upon discovering that all the Vhorishkovas were werewolves, he slaughtered them all. His final victim was an ancient, shriveled, toothless wolfman who begged for mercy. His pleas fell on deaf ears.

The slaughter of the Vhorishkovas left Weathermay fundamentally changed. His affinity for animals seemed to have left him, and in its place was a cold lump of hatred. While his fight against evil had been a central part of his life until that point, it became an all-consuming crusade afterward.

Weathermay has not returned to Mordent since the incident nine years ago, instead taking up residence in Arbora. This southeastern Nova Vaasan city is located about as far away from Mordent as possible. He still roams the Core, and more than ever, the mere mention of his name causes those who serve evil to shudder in fear.

Personality

Earlier in his life, Weathermay was shy and awkward when dealing with others. Among men, he became nervous and often spoke out of turn or said the wrong thing. In the company of women, especially pretty ones, he stuttered and became almost comical. For those reasons, Weathermay had as little to do with the people he protected as possible.

Now, however, others shun Weathermay instead of the other way around. Now, he projects a sense of barely controlled rage that makes everyone around him uneasy. Where before he would attempt to carry on conversations, he now speaks only when he requires information from someone.

When on the trail of a target, Weathermay is a relentless tracker who rests only when it becomes apparent that his horse or rare traveling companions need to rest. Once he has a quarry in his sights, he does not abandon the hunt until it is slain. Pleas for mercy go unheeded, and those who attempt to force themselves between Weathermay and his victims forfeit their own lives—unless they can swiftly prove to him that his intended target is not the evil being he believes it to be.

For Weathermay, there are only two types of beings—good and evil. One he is sworn to protect, the other he destroys without hesitation. The memory of Gennifer's bleeding form still haunts his dreams every night.

Combat

When he engages in battle, Weathermay depends on two weapons. The first of these is *Gossamer*, a

George Weathermay

magical *long sword +2*. This weapon is specially enchanted for use against the incorporeal undead, allowing it to harm ghosts and other such spirits even if a +2 weapon would normally lack the enchantment to do so. Weathermay also carries a short sword.

Although no longer a ranger, Weathermay continues to fight with two weapons, suffering the appropriate –1 penalty with the first weapon and a –3 penalty on the second weapon. (He uses *Gossamer* as his primary weapon, so its enchantment cancels out the attack penalty.)

Despite the loss of his special abilities, he is nonetheless so skilled in fighting with two weapons that he can opt to attack with the axe or use it in defense, gaining a +1 bonus to his Armor Class.

Equipment

Weathermay travels in the company of his horse, Shadowchaser, and his two hounds, Cerberus and Artemis. These dogs have been trained specifically to track lycanthropes.

Weathermay's saddle contains three secret compartments, containing two silver daggers, a holy symbol, and a vial of holy water. He usually also hides additional weapons and useful items on his person.

Adventure Ideas

For nearly a decade now, Weathermay has been pursuing Natalia Vhorishkova throughout the Core. She is a fearless werewolf driven by a lust for blood and pain that even she does not understand. Even more importantly, she is the single foe who has repeatedly evaded Weathermay. She remains one step ahead of him, leaving him with a cold trail long before he can catch up with her.

Player characters pursuing a particularly brutal werewolf may cross paths with Weathermay, as he investigates whether or not the attacks can again put him on Natalia's trail. If they are indeed hunting the beauteous werebeast, she may try to outsmart the hunters by secretly befriending or seducing one of the player characters. She would then attack him, hoping to taunt Weathermay with the similarity to her betrayal of his affections years ago. She will not kill the character, however. Her goal is to merely infect him with lycanthropy.

Another possibility arises with Weathermay's twin nieces, Gennifer and Laurie Weathermay-Foxgrove. They have been watching over the interests of Rudolph van Richten since his disappearance in 750, and these two adventurous

and inquisitive young women will eventually begin an active investigation of his fate. Player characters who have played through the events of the *Bleak House* boxed set will eventually be tracked down by the pair. They will attempt to convince the characters to return with them to the Van Richten estate so they can complete their investigation.

Gennifer and Laurie, however, attract the attention of others who want to find Van Richten—old enemies who want revenge, like Natalia Vhorishkova and Emil Bollenbach. They and the player characters will be pursued by a variety of shadowy figures, at least one of whom will have Weathermay on his trail. When he catches up with the group, the twins will be surprised and disturbed by the change that has come over their uncle since they last saw him, as children. With the optimism of youth, they convince him to assist in their investigation into the fate of Van Richten.

At some point, they could confide to a particularly heroic character (such as a paladin or ranger) that they hope Weathermay will remember the kind of hero he was when they were growing up, and perhaps return to that due to player character's example. Their attempt to restore Weathermay to the way they remember him can be a complicated subplot in an ongoing campaign. Whether Weathermay returns fully to the path of goodness, or continues his slide into darkness, is up to the Dungeon Master.

Ideally, any character who tries to help Weathermay should find himself caught up in the old traveler's world. The Dungeon Master should lead the helpful character (and his party) on adventures that seem to vindicate Weathermay's bitterness and obsession. (For example, while the party joins the great lycanthrope tracker on a hunt, his cherished henchman of many years could die horribly.) A good RAVENLOFT adventure entices the heroes to look into the darkness they oppose, and see how they could just as easily slip into it. After the thrill of successfully hunting a couple werebeasts wears off, it should occur to the adventurers that Weathermay is more savage than his quarry. Those who share his gusto may be called upon to make powers checks.

George Weathermay may be used to introduce the monster hunter kit to an interested player character. Of course, the monster type is the lycanthrope, but the Dungeon Master can rule that not all wereforms are allowed. The player character who wants to adopt the kit must accompany Weathermay on two successful hunts.